"And what am I?"

"Don't tempt me," Anne threatened.

"Oh, come on. You've been perfectly free with your insulting opinions of me so far. Why stop now?"

"You're intelligent, strong, utterly independent and self-confident to the point of arrogance." She frankly listed the personal assets she found so irritating.

Hunter's square mouth tilted slowly in amusement. "You forgot handsome."

SUSAN NAPIER was born on St. Valentine's Day, so it's not surprising she has developed an enduring love of romantic stories. She started her writing career as a journalist in Auckland, New Zealand, trying her hand at romance fiction only after she had married her handsome boss! Numerous books later she still lives with her most enduring hero, two future heroes—her sons!—two cats and a computer. When she's not writing she likes to read and cook, often simultaneously!

Books by Susan Napier

HARLEQUIN PRESENTS
1554—SECRET ADMIRER
1595—WINTER OF DREAMS
1616—THE HAWK AND THE LAMB
1674—THE CRUELLEST LIE
1707—PHANTOM LOVER
1744—SAVAGE COURTSHIP

SUSAN NAPIER

The Sister Swap

Harlequin Books

TORONTO • NEW YORK • LONDON
AMSTERDAM • PARIS • SYDNEY • HAMBURG
STOCKHOLM • ATHENS • TOKYO • MILAN
MADRID • WARSAW • BUDAPEST • AUCKLAND

ISBN 0-373-11788-4

THE SISTER SWAP

First North American Publication 1996.

CHAPTER ONE

THE loud, driving rock music shook the rafters and vibrated through the hardwood floor, sending a delicious hum up through Anne's bones as she danced joyously around the room in her bare feet.

She extended her arms above her head, clicking her fingers in time to the raucous beat as she moved with the increasing frenzy of the music. The long rope of red-brown hair whipped around her hips as she took a running leap through the shaft of late afternoon summer sunshine that slanted in through the big windows at one end of the long room, landing with a dramatic thump beside the random stacks of cardboard cartons that held her belongings. Anticipating the approaching climactic crescendo, she performed two more exuberant leaping turns and had launched into a third when she was suddenly left hanging by the abrupt cessation of her musical support.

Anne landed awkwardly, her heartbeat accelerating as she whirled to face the man who had wrenched out the plug from the portable music-centre that sat on the high bench that separated the rest of the room from the small kitchen area.

He was tall and bullishly big, chest and thighs bulging against the unfashionably tight, faded blue T-shirt and jeans he wore. The expression on his face was as bullish as the rest of him, black eyebrows lowered over glowering dark eyes.

'What did you do that for?' Anne panted nervously, as much from apprehension as from her wild exertions.

The open door behind him testified to her careless stupidity. The taxi-van driver who had kindly helped carry her boxes up six flights of stairs had departed half an hour ago and she was aware that the warehouse below was empty after four-thirty. There was no one to run to her aid if she screamed.

Suddenly all the cautionary tales she had laughingly dismissed about the big, bad city came back to haunt her. She had even forgotten the first basic rule—to lock her door!

'You mean why did I shut down that shrieking racket?' came the snarling reply. 'I would have thought that was bloody obvious. I've been pounding at your door for five minutes!'

Anne relaxed slightly. He was certainly angry but if his intentions were violent he would have welcomed the loud music and shouted lyrics as a handy cover for her screams. She took a few steps towards him and then stopped, freshly aware of the disparity in their sizes.

At five feet four she liked to think she was of average height for a woman, but the closer she got to this colossus, the more aware she was of the slenderness of her build. She had a wiry strength concealed within her fragile-looking femininity but she was wise enough to know its limits. She would have to assert herself with her intellect rather than her physical person.

'That "shrieking racket",' she began firmly, 'happens to be one of the finest rock groups in the——'

'I don't care if it's Kiri Te Kanawa and the Paris Opera.' Her invader dropped the plug on top of the dead radio and adopted the quintessential threatening male attitude, fists on hips. 'I don't like having music rammed down my throat at ninety decibels——'

'Your ears,' corrected Anne absently, thinking that the man would probably be quite handsome if he didn't scowl like that, in a way that engraved the lines of experience in the olive skin into a vivid warning sign: Here lurks bad temper!

His eyes weren't just dark, she discovered as he continued to glower at her, they were as black as midnight, the same colour as the thick, shaggy, collar-length hair swept back from his broad forehead. He was somewhere in his mid-thirties, she guessed, and life had delivered enough knocks to turn him into a tough customer. His chin was so square you could chisel rock with it and his rectangular mouth looked just as cutting. Anne was pleased with her mental description and she smiled, which only made him frown even more as he barked, 'What?'

'I think you mixed your metaphors. You mean rammed into your ears, not down your throat. You don't hear with your mouth.'

'Then why did your infernal racket turn my stomach?' he growled sardonically before adding impatiently, 'I didn't come here for a damned language lecture——'

'If you're going to keep using offensive language, I'm sorry, but I'm going to have to ask you to leave,' said Anne primly. She had never reacted well to being barked at, especially by big, arrogant males.

He made a sound deep in his large chest, like the approaching rumble of a freight train. 'I have no intention of staying——'

'Then why did you come?'

'To tell you to shut the hell up!'

Anne's own impulsive temper began to build up steam. 'Is your vocabulary so stunted you can't express yourself without swearing?'

'That's rich, coming from you!' he shot back. 'That rock singer you're so impressed with was shrieking out far worse at the top of his lungs.'

Anne had the grace to blush. 'Well—er—the music puts it in a different context,' she said weakly.

'Oh, I see. You don't mind being cursed at, as long as it's to music.'

She was beginning to get the uncomfortable feeling that this hulking man might be able to run intellectual as well as physical rings around her. She was nervous enough about her move from a tiny rural town to the huge, sprawling city of Auckland and the new life she was embarking on, especially fraught as it was with guilty secrets. She didn't need any additional undermining of her confidence. Katlin had been bad enough. Her elder sister had deeply impressed on Anne the dire consequences of being found out in their deception, at the same time hastily assuring her that the chances of discovery were infinitesimal . . . as long as Anne kept a cool head. Easier said than done.

'Look, would you mind stating your business——?'

'I thought I had.'

Anne frowned, her fly-away brows losing their faintly surprised natural arch. 'You mean about the noise?' Suddenly the light dawned. 'Oh, are you from downstairs?' That would explain the bulging muscles. The men she had seen in the docking bay of the warehouse when she had arrived had been heaving about enormous crates as if they were made of marshmallow. 'I thought everyone in the warehouse knocked off at four, and anyway, I can't believe that sound from here would travel——'

'Not the warehouse. I live in the apartment next door,' he snapped, jerking a thumb over his shoulder at the open door. 'And, believe me, the sound travels between the two all too well.'

Anne's mouth dropped open. 'Next door? But you can't be.' Her voice rose accusingly. 'Nobody said anything about there being anyone else living here!'

Quite the reverse, in fact. She had been shown around the sparsely furnished loft atop the warehouse building by a representative from the foundation which had awarded the year-long grant. The man had given Anne the distinct impression that she would be totally alone and undisturbed in her cosy eyrie close to the sprawling city campus of Auckland University. He certainly hadn't mentioned any surly, beetle-browed neighbour. The fact that she would have no interfering fellow-residents poking their curious noses into her life and work had been the deciding factor in her agreeing to fulfil the conditions of the grant. Now this, when it was too late to back out!

Thank God she had put her foot down over the money that went along with the grant—at least her conscience was clear on *that* score. Katlin had wanted to give her the majority of the modest monthly pension, but Anne had adamantly refused to accept anything more than direct expenses, of which she kept a very strict account, just in case there were any official questions later. For herself, Anne was using the precious savings that she had accrued over the years from selling eggs, honey and vegetables at the family farm gate.

'Perhaps they assumed we wouldn't notice each other,' he said sarcastically. 'Fat chance if you intend to run a one-woman disco at all hours of the day and night...'

Anne's mouth snapped shut to stop herself saying something equally rude. Live and let live was her motto. If they were neighbours then she'd just have to try and make the best of it.

'Hardly at all hours, since I've only just moved in. I was just celebrating, that's all,' she said in her normal, soft, conciliatory tones.

The reply she received was bluntly non-conciliatory. 'Well, celebrate quietly in future. The walls here are paper-thin. And cut out the acrobatics. These floorboards run almost the length of the whole upper floor. Vibrations travel as effectively as noise.'

Anne's hazel eyes narrowed. 'Then you'd better get shock-absorbers as well as ear-muffs because I dance to keep fit.'

That led the fierce black gaze to wander down over her huge, baggy, less-than-pure-white T-shirt and calf-length purple cotton leggings with the little darned patch on her knee.

'Fit for what?' The rag-bag, was the suggestion in his dismissive gaze.

'To stand up to bullies like you,' she snapped. 'Now you've performed your neighbourly act of welcome, would you mind shutting the door behind you? And next time don't come in until you're invited!'

'There won't be a next time. As far as you're concerned no one else *does* live in this building, understand?'

Anne blinked. She understood all right. He was insinuating that she might pester him with unwanted attentions... after he had come thrusting his way into *her* attention! 'I won't bother you as long as you don't bother me!' she told him. 'For your information, Mr—Mr whoever-you-are——'

'Lewis. Hunter Lewis, Miss Tremaine.' He glared at her as if he expected to be challenged over his name, and she was momentarily side-tracked from her righteous indignation.

'How do you know who I am?'

'You're the Markham Grant.'

That took the wind out of her sails. The private grant scheme was very low-key and had received no publicity beyond a brief announcement in a literary magazine, the aim being to create a totally unpressured environment in which a writer could work. Was it coincidence that he knew of it, or was he in some way connected with the foundation? Her heart sank at the thought.

'Oh. Are you here on a grant too?' she asked cautiously.

'No, I'm not,' he snapped, as if she had insulted him. 'And I'm surprised they're handing them out like lollies to children these days.' He gave her brightly mismatched outfit another contemptuous study.

'Whatever happened to the concept of struggle and suffering for the sake of one's art? If every new writer got provided with a cushy number in his or her creative infanthood we'd have a generation of writers producing work with as much emotional depth as the telephone directory!'

The door had swung shut behind him before Anne could recover from her shock at the scathing attack. Belatedly she rushed over and flung it open again, just in time to see him duck through a door under the short flight of stairs at the end of the corridor which led to a small, flat section of the roof. She had noticed the door previously but had assumed from its battered appearance and narrow dimensions that it was some kind of caretaker's store-room.

'Well!' she exclaimed disgustedly, annoyed that she hadn't been quick enough to come up with some pithy little comment that would have hurried him on his way. Not that he'd needed any hurrying. He evidently couldn't get away from her fast enough.

She turned back to survey her new home and was jolted out of her preoccupation by the sound of slow applause.

'Oh, my gosh!' She rushed over to the boxes, pushing them apart until she discovered her concealed audience. The applause was slow because every second clap failed to connect, the owner of the hands not quite having the co-ordination to match his enthusiasm.

'Oh, Ivan, I forgot all about you!' She snatched up the chubby baby, horrified by her lapse in attention. 'What did you crawl in there for? Did that nasty man frighten you?'

Ivan's face crunched up and for one horrifying moment his rumpled, downy black eyebrows and narrowed dark eyes actually resembled those of the obnoxious Hunter Lewis. Ivan even had the same midnight-black hair...

But no—Anne brought her panicked speculations to a screeching halt. He thought Anne was Katlin Tremaine, so he had never met her striking sister. Besides, Katlin said Ivan's father was Russian. Hunter Lewis might have the temperament of a marauding Cossack but his accents were definitely Kiwi!

The strangely disturbing thought of that hulking brute as the father of her innocent little godson made Anne hug him tightly and he let out a squawk of protest.

'Sorry. We won't talk about that bad man. We won't even think about him, will we? Now, what are we going to unpack next, Ivan? You show me. Point to a box...'

The active assistance of a seven-month-old wasn't conducive to efficiency and it took a long time for Anne to organise her rather meagre possessions. Since the loft was furnished, albeit rather sparsely, she hadn't needed to bring much, but she couldn't have left her books at home and then there was all the considerable paraphernalia required to keep Ivan the Terrible happy, healthy and occupied.

Most of that she took into the small bedroom at the windowless end of the main room and while she was there, assembling, with her usual lack of mechanical genius, the portable baby Easi-cot—'Easy, my foot!' she grumbled to Ivan as he busily babbled incoherent advice as to how to connect point D with section 2—she was distracted from her task by a sound on the other side of the wall. Music.

She scrambled up over the narrow bed and pressed her ear against the painted surface. Jazz.

'Well, of all the cheek!' She was almost tempted to go out and turn her own tape back on, even louder than before, but she had to concede that he didn't appear to have the volume very high. Then she heard another sound, a very familiar electronic tap-tapping.

'He's got a typewriter.' She looked down at Ivan in consternation. He grinned back, showing all six teeth. 'Oh, no! Ivan, what if he's a writer too?' Overwhelmed with dismay, she slumped beside him on the floor. Ivan began to laugh his piping little shrill and she leapt up again, conscious of those listening walls. 'No, no, darling—shush!'

Anne tucked Ivan under her arm and scurried back out to the big room, her heart beating like a drum. 'We mustn't let the bad man hear you,' she admonished him, one finger held in front of her lips as she placed him in his high chair in the kitchenette and began to forage in the refrigerator. 'If there's one thing crabby old hermits hate more than loud rock music it's crying babies. So you will be good while we're here, won't you, darling?'

Ivan issued a scornful babble at her words, as well he might. The Terrible was Anne's purely ironic nickname. Ivan was the most friendly, good-natured and well-behaved baby in the world. In fact, he was enough to make a capable adult feel inferior. Sometimes Anne felt as if he was not really a baby at all, but a computer-generated ideal. He didn't dribble, he never threw up his food or cried for no apparent reason; he even messed his nappies in the tidiest possible fashion. You could set the clock by his naps and he had slept through the night since he was four weeks old. If it weren't for the fact that he couldn't walk or talk for himself Anne would almost feel superfluous to his well-ordered existence!

While Ivan amused himself by painting on a Charlie Chaplin moustache with a disintegrating rusk smothered with his favourite Vegemite spread, Anne whipped them both up an omelette for dinner, adding extra cheese to her own and herbs from the garden pots that her father had carefully packed in a wooden crate with plenty of damp newspaper for the flight north.

She sat on a stool at the breakfast-bar to eat hers, revelling in the peace as she popped the occasional spoonful from Ivan's bunny-plate into his mouth while he diligently helped out with his fists, chuckling as the mixture squelched out from the bottom of his chubby fist on to his cotton bib.

Back at home mealtimes were always rowdy affairs, with her mother and father and her four brothers always competing to air their cheerful opinions. They were a very close-knit and gregarious family, except for Katlin, who at twenty-eight was the eldest, and had chosen to move off the small, isolated South Island family farm while still in her late teens and live in virtual seclusion in order to write. Ivan's arrival on the scene had been a cataclysmic upheaval in her solitary life. As usual it had been her more responsible sister who had been left holding the baby... this time literally!

Anne grinned to herself as she mopped up Ivan's efforts at feeding himself with a damp cloth. A big city and a small baby were hardly what most people would see as a peaceful combination, but for Anne it was the realisation of a dream and she intended to make the most of it. Just a simple thing like having what *she* wanted for dinner instead of what would sustain gargantuan farm appetites gave her a magnificent sense of independence.

She gave Ivan the bottle of milk which rounded off his meal and then sat him down on the floor to play with his plastic blocks while she dragged the lop-sided cot out of the bedroom and finished assembling it. By the time she managed to attach the wheels correctly Ivan was looking heavy-eyed, and sucking his thumb, a sure indication that he was tired. No doubt his incredibly accurate internal clock had told him it was past his bedtime but, true to type, he wasn't complaining.

She bathed him in the kitchen sink since the tiny bathroom which opened off the kitchen—obviously for the convenience of the plumber rather than the tenant—only possessed a shower, toilet and small basin, but Ivan didn't seem to mind. He kicked and splashed merrily, briefly regaining his liveliness, before dozing as she patted him dry and put on his thick night-nappy and stretchy sleep-suit.

He was asleep almost before his head hit the mattress, his hands clutching the fuzzy pink stuffed pig that was his prized possession. She kissed him on his button nose, a flood of tenderness warming her with contentment as she softly sang him his bedtime song and then quietly wheeled the cot through to the bedroom.

She tiptoed back out to the living-room and plumped herself down on the high, polished-cotton couch, pleased that it was long enough for her to stretch out full-length. There was also an easy-chair, a large bean-bag and four spindle-backed chairs around the oval wooden dining-table to choose from. At home it was a battle for the best sitting space in the evenings. A wooden roll-topped desk on which Anne had set her typewriter, a small coffee-table and a large bookcase were the only other furnishings in the room apart from a few scattered rugs on the bare floorboards.

The man from the foundation had been slightly apologetic that there was no television but Anne didn't mind. She had her small music-centre and anyway she intended to be too busy to be a mere spectator of life from now on. There was no telephone either, which had given her a few qualms at first, but there was a phone box just up the street and she could appreciate that the usual grant recipients preferred to be incommunicado while they were beavering over their manuscripts.

She lay on the couch, *her* couch, listening to the muted sounds of the city, then she got up, dissatisfied, and dragged the heavy piece of furniture over to the arched windows. She had earlier opened the curved upper portions of the window with the long wooden window-hook and now she folded back the lower, rectangular segments. With the couch angled just right she could lie on it and look out at the last orange glow of the sun as it curtsied behind the jumble of city buildings. As the twilight turned to dusk she was able to see the lights burning at the entrance to the art school, and behind it in the multi-storeyed school of engineering. Across the road were the other main buildings, the library and theatre and administration blocks. Soon she would be a part of the stream of students that came and went each day from that campus city-within-a-city.

Fired with a fresh wave of enthusiasm, Anne made herself a cup of tea and got out the course leaflets and introductory material that the university had sent her when she had enrolled in her language courses. She had several days to familiarise herself with the city and make arrangements for Ivan's day-care before orientation week started, but she intended to be well-prepared for her first foray into higher education. She had already purchased some of the basic required texts and she added them to the little pile and made herself comfortable on the couch.

She was reading about the gender endings of Russian nouns when the pendent lights overhead flickered once and then went out.

The dark wasn't complete because of the street-lighting outside but it was enough to disorientate Anne as she tried to negotiate the shadowy loft, trying to remember if the man from the foundation had mentioned a fuse-box. She checked the refrigerator, just to make sure that it wasn't just the light bulbs that had blown, but the light inside wasn't operating either so she began opening cupboards and muttering to herself when the logical places didn't yield anything that looked like a junction-box.

The longer she searched, the more unpalatable became the most sensible solution to her problem. She could just go to bed and deal with it in the morning, of course, but she wouldn't have hot water again until the following evening if the mains switch wasn't re-set before morning. Maybe it was more than just her own problem anyway.

She cheered up at the thought that Hunter Lewis's electricity might have gone off as well. A trouble shared was a trouble halved, and he wouldn't be able to blame her if the whole floor was out.

She crept into the bedroom to listen to Ivan's steady little snore, and frowned as she heard the tap-tap and the music still filtering through the wall.

Oh, well, at least she knew he was at home and still awake!

But in no better a mood, she realised five minutes later when he flung open his door and glared at her.

No wonder his door was so battered; he must be hell on joinery! she thought to herself as she smiled hopefully at him in the dimly lit passageway.

'I wonder if you could help me——?'

'No.'

'My electricity has gone off and I don't know where the fuse-box is located,' she continued calmly as if he hadn't spoken.

'God defend me from helpless women!' he said through his teeth.

'Why, are you too feeble to defend yourself?'

'Very funny!

'Then why aren't you smiling?' She threw up a hand. 'No, don't tell me, let me guess. You smiled once and the sky fell on you. Well, Chicken Little, you can stop panicking now. All I want is a light and the fuse-box.'

'And fuse-wire, and a screwdriver, and——'

'Are you naturally this obnoxious, or is it something you've specially trained for?'

'Look, lady, I didn't ask you to come thumping on my door——'

'I didn't ask you to come thumping at mine either, Mr Lewis, but you did. So we're even. Now, are you capable of answering one simple question without turning it into a tiresome lecture? Do you know where the fuse-box for my apartment is located?'

For an answer he shut the door in her face and she was just about to scream it down when he reopened it carrying a small toolkit. He looked down at her furiously flushed face, small clenched fists and bare toes curled with rage and, wonder of wonders, produced a slight smile that bracketed the rectangular mouth with deep lines.

'Temper, temper!'

'You can talk!' she said tartly, fascinated in spite of herself. He didn't look all that much different when he smiled, she realised in amusement. He still looked broodingly dangerous, his black eyes smouldering with hostility and suspicion, their hooded lids giving them a predatory quality.

He didn't answer, turning his back and walking towards the stairs. Anne got the impression that he did that a lot—turned his back on people.

At the head of the main flight of wooden stairs a sensor turned on a light on the first landing down, revealing a small cupboard in the wall which proved to contain odds and ends of tools and cleaning equipment—and fuse-boxes numbered for both apartments.

'Thank you.' Anne waited for him to get out of the way. 'Excuse me.' She tapped him on the shoulder as he pulled out the rectangular fuses, checking them. Her finger practically bounced off the armoured muscle. Anne's four brothers were well-built—even Mike who was still only fourteen was much bigger than she was—so she wasn't usually impressed by male bulk, but this one was built like a tank.

'Hold this.'

She ignored the screwdriver.

'Look, Mr Lewis, I do know how to change a fuse——'

'Hold this.'

'No.'

He turned his head. In profile his nose looked every bit as arrogantly prominent as the rest of him. 'Haven't you ever been told not to look a gift-horse in the mouth?'

Her eyes shifted to his wide, straight mouth and for no particular reason she felt herself flushing.

'I've also been warned about Greeks bearing gifts,' she said hurriedly.

'I'm not Greek,' he commented, tucking the screwdriver between his teeth and turning back to his task.

'You're not a horse either.' Except maybe the rear end of one! she added silently. 'If you'll just step aside I'll handle my own problems.'

'And risk you botching it up so you have to come simpering back to my door again? No, thanks.'

'I've never simpered in my life!' she fumed, eyeing the stiched denim pockets below the black leather belt. One good, hard kick to that tightly packed rear and she would feel a whole lot better.

'Don't even think about it, country girl. I'm not only bigger than you, I'm faster.'

He hadn't even looked around and she was furious at him for guessing what she was thinking, as well as for that mocking dig about her origins. What chance had she to hide anything if he had such acutely perceptive instincts?

'Yes—at jumping to conclusions. Tell me, what brought on this powerful paranoia you have regarding women? I can't figure out why you think you're such an irresistible dish that you have to warn off total strangers. As a "country girl" I've seen plenty of beef on the hoof and, believe me, you're over-pricing yourself.'

He snapped the repaired fuse back into place and depressed the trip-switch before he backed out of the cupboard, forcing her to retreat. 'That smart mouth of yours is going to get you into trouble one day.'

They were back to mouths again. Now he had turned and was looking at hers and she tightened it deliberately, knowing that her full lower lip tended to give a false impression of sultriness.

'Is that a threat?' She bristled under the insolent black stare.

'More in the nature of kindly advice.'

'Kindly!' she snorted. '*You*?'

'Don't try and provoke me more than you already have, Miss Tremaine,' he drawled in that aggravatingly warm voice that was so at odds with his manner. 'I suppose I'd better check that everything is working...'

Before she realised what he had meant he was up the stairs and heading towards her half-open door. His boast about moving fast hadn't been idle. Frantically trying to remember whether she had tidied everything away after putting Ivan to bed, Anne flew up after him, and nipped in front just in time to bar his entry with one slender arm across the doorway.

'The lights are on so obviously everything's OK,' she said breathlessly, trying to act casually as his momentum brought his chest up against her restraining arm.

He froze and she smiled brilliantly at him. 'Thank you ever so much for your help,' she gushed. 'I don't know what I would have done without you.'

He was looking at her oddly, through thoughtfully narrowed eyes, and she instantly realised that she was overdoing the gratitude. After the scathing comments she had just flung at him he was bound to be suspicious of such a sudden *volte face*. 'You can go back to—er—whatever you were doing now,' she urged more calmly. 'I don't want to put you to any more trouble...'

To her dismay he shrugged. 'No trouble.' He leaned forward as he spoke and she felt the straining pressure of that deep chest against her upper arm.

'No, really, there's no need!' she squeaked desperately as he lifted a big hand and effortlessly brushed her restraining limb aside.

Three steps into the room he stopped, crossing his hands over his chest as he slowly surveyed the territory. Coming up beside him, Anne was relieved to see that there was nothing untoward in the scene. Relief brought back her courage. 'Satisfied?' she demanded defiantly.

'At the very least, from your state of guilty panic, I expected to find an orgy going on in here,' he murmured, confirming her opinion of his acumen. Worse than a nosy neighbour was a suspicious one who could read your mind like a book!

'I'm sorry to disappoint you.'

'Oh, you haven't disappointed me, Miss Tremaine. My expectations of you aren't high enough for that to be possible. I expect the worst, and if you don't oblige then I can only be pleasantly surprised.'

'What a ghastly philosophy of life!' Anne stared at him disapprovingly. 'No wonder you're so bad-tempered. So would I be if I went around in a constant state of gloomy pessimism.'

'Yes, I can see that you're one of life's noisy optimists,' he said drily. 'Relentlessly determined to enjoy yourself at all costs.'

'Only a pessimist could make optimism sound depressing,' was Anne's tart reply. 'And one person's noise is music to another person's ears.'

'I'm a realist, not a pessimist, but we won't get into an argument about it.'

'Why not? Afraid you'd lose?'

'I have better things to do with my time than argue semantics with starry-eyed Lolitas——'

'Lolita! I'll have you know I'm twenty——' She stopped herself just in time and added haughtily, 'I'm older than I look and I was never starry-eyed. Now that you've assured yourself you're not missing out on an orgy, perhaps you'll finally go back to where you belong.'

He gave her a small, ironic inclination of his head. 'Ah, would that I knew where that was...'

She almost softened, intrigued by that weary, cryptic murmur, except that she saw the deep, hooded gleam in his eyes and suddenly knew that he was playing on her compassion deliberately, slyly proving his point about her unsophisticated gullibility.

'Try hell,' she said sweetly. 'I'm sure people often direct you that way.'

A startled stillness gripped his expression, then he threw back his head and laughed, the warm sound rising richly to the high, sloping rafters. His eyes slitted and all the brooding lines of his face seemed to lift with the upward curve of his mouth. She had certainly been right about his handsomeness when he wasn't scowling. Suddenly his cynical suspicion of a strange woman invading his personal space didn't seem quite so untenable.

'I don't know what you're laughing at—it wasn't a compliment,' she pointed out. 'You know, for someone so inordinately keen to be left alone you're singularly difficult to get rid of!'

His laughter ended as abruptly as it had begun and he gave her a slow, measuring look as he began to saunter towards the door in his own sweet time. 'Such big, pompous words for such a little country girl.'

'Size and geographical origin has nothing whatever to do with intelligence,' she said icily. 'And I'm a *woman*, not a girl.'

'That remains to be seen.'

'But not by *you*!'

This time she got to shut the door smartly in *his* face, although her satisfaction was somewhat dimmed by the memory of that last, grimly taunting smile.

It seemed to say that Hunter Lewis would see whatever he wanted to see, whenever he damned well wanted to see it.

She would just have to keep well out of his way and make sure he never got the opportunity.

CHAPTER TWO

'I THINK they should call it *disorientation* week!' Anne groaned as she collapsed with her small backpack on to a seat in the university quad.

'Decided to give up and go home to the farm?' grinned the plump blonde already sitting there as she carefully added a dollop of cream from her doughnut to a paper cup of coffee.

'Are you kidding? I'm having a great time!' Anne rallied. 'It's just taking me longer than I thought to find my way around this maze.'

She stretched out her legs in their age-softened jeans, enjoying the cool breeze playing about the loose neckline of the white shirt that Mike had grown out of six months ago. It had been part of the dress uniform at her brother's school but her mother had added a jaunty feminine touch with embroidery along the pocket and collar. With sleeves rolled up and shirt-tails hanging out Anne had felt confident of blending in with her fellow students, despite the fact that she was older than most of the other first-years.

'Don't worry, even second-year students like me still get lost sometimes,' Rachel Blake told her sympathetically. She had cheerfully admitted to being a student dilettante whose wealthy parents could afford for her to dabble at university for as long as it took her to get a degree—any degree.

To Anne, who loved to study but had to watch every cent of expenditure, it sounded like an existence to be envied, and yet she didn't. Such aimlessness was a waste of time and effort and Anne didn't want to waste a single moment of her time at university. Her aim was to gain her degree in the shortest possible time without overloading herself to the point where she didn't have enough free time to earn the extra money essential to the continuation of her studies. After that, the world was her oyster!

'At least you have the stamina for all the trekking about we have to do,' Rachel added, with a mocking glance down at her own full figure. 'You country girls probably have the strength of marathon runners from chasing all those sheep up and down the alps.'

Anne grinned. 'Our farm's nowhere near the Southern Alps and the dogs did all the running. I just leaned on the gates and whistled.'

Her new friend's use of the phrase 'country girl' sent a small *frisson* up her spine. In the past two weeks she had seen very little of her surly neighbour, mainly because she had adopted a policy of active avoidance. Apart from the occasional thunderous knocking on the wall whenever she forgot herself and played her tapes a little too loud, or to cover one of Ivan's rare bouts of crying, he was just as scrupulous at avoiding contact.

Whatever it was that Hunter Lewis did for a living, his hours seemed to be erratic, so that it was no easy task to work out a schedule by which she could be sure of missing him whenever she ventured out. However, an ear to her bedroom wall was usually enough to ascertain if he was at home and therefore unlikely to be encountered on the stairs. Coming back in she just had to keep a sharp look-out and take her chances. Every time she went up or down the stairs it was an adventure, and her heart pounded in her throat with nervous apprehension.

'So... how's the rest of your lecture schedule shaping up? I can't believe you're taking Japanese *and* Russian. One language at a time is enough for most of us!'

Anne shrugged. 'I've already done basic correspondence courses in them so it won't be too much of a shock. I used to love making up and solving codes and cryptograms when I was a kid. I even used to invent languages with proper alphabets and rules of grammar... put the whole works down in little notebooks. It's just something that I'm good at.'

'Inventing *grammar*? Now I *know* you're weird.' Rachel rolled her eyes. 'Most of us spend our childhood trying to avoid having to write any grammar! Your teachers must have loved you. So... what do you think of your lecturers so far?'

'They seem OK.' It was an understatement. Just to be at university was wonderful and Anne knew she was seeing everything through rose-coloured spectacles.

'Lucky you. I've got some killers from last year. Him for example.' She screwed up her face and inclined her head at one of the figures crossing the quad. 'Gorgeous bod, personality of Dracula. You know, there are poor souls who actually take political studies because they think it's going to be an easy option. Big mistake. The drop-out rate in his class is fierce. He has a fiendish temper and he just piles on the assignments!'

'So how come you're still taking it, then? Can't resist the gorgeous bod?' teased Anne with a smile as she casually scanned the quad.

'I discovered I'm actually quite good at it,' admitted Rachel sheepishly, making Anne laugh. 'I know, I know... it shocked me even more than it did Professor Lewis. He thought I was just another blonde bimbo looking to plug a hole in my schedule—practically shredded me to pieces that first semester. The Pit Bull, I call him... let him scent a weakness and those big jaws just go *chomp*!'

Anne wasn't listening. She had spotted him at the exact moment that Rachel had mentioned his name. He was walking towards them at an oblique angle but there was no mistaking that tight, impatient stride or the saturnine expression. He was wearing a sports jacket over dark trousers and pale shirt and tie, and was carrying a bulging leather briefcase.

'*Professor* Lewis? Professor *Hunter* Lewis?' she said hollowly, hoping against hope that it was merely a ghastly coincidence.

'Yeah. You know him?'

'He's a lecturer *here*?'

'I told you, political studies.' To her horror Rachel lifted her hand and waved to the man as he approached to pass their seated figures. 'Hi, Hunter.'

She received a grunt in reply and a brief glance that didn't even break his stride. Anne was relaxing again when the big head suddenly snapped back around and he came to a halt. Before he could beat her to it Anne scowled at him. As if it weren't enough that she had to avoid him around the flat, now she was going to have to worry about running into him on campus as well.

To her dismay he backed up, ignoring his student, and stared at Anne. 'What are you doing here?' he snapped.

As if it had anything to do with him!

'Following you, of course,' she snapped back, flicking her long plait back between her defiantly stiff shoulder-blades.

His face darkened. 'What in the hell for?'

He believed her! The incredible egotism of the man. 'I'm a masochist. I'm hoping if I throw myself in your path often enough you'll fall in love with me and invite me to live miserably with you ever after.'

Anne heard Rachel's soft gasp, but ignored it in favour of maintaining her defiant front. He wasn't *her* professor. To her he was just an obnoxious stranger.

'Is that supposed to be a joke?'

'Not to someone who doesn't have a sense of humour.'

He didn't dispute the point, instead abruptly switching tactics. 'Are you taking an extension course here at the university?' he asked more politely.

Ah, it was finally beginning to sink in that her life might not revolve entirely around him. She widened her eyes innocently. 'Actually I'm thinking of enrolling in political studies.'

A brief spark of emotion glowed in the hooded gaze and then Anne was subjected to a long, silent look that would have made her blush if she hadn't been so annoyed. 'Sorry, my class already has a waiting-list,' he said with silky insincerity.

'Oh, dear, and I'm sure there won't be any vacancies opening up when the term is under way and your students realise what a sweet-tempered and tolerant being you really are behind that gruff exterior.'

This time Rachel gave her a sharp nudge of her elbow in the kidneys and Anne felt guilty for allowing her temper to get the better of her discretion.

The dark gaze switched from Anne to Rachel's flushed and curious face. 'Been telling tales out of school, Rachel?'

'Wouldn't dream of it, Professor,' said Rachel with glib mock-deference.

'Oh, be my guest,' he responded mildly. 'I'd much rather have the wheat sorted from the chaff before the first lecture.'

'The chaff being those who don't treat every utterance of yours as a pearl of indisputable wisdom, I suppose,' Anne murmured.

'I'm surprised at a country girl mixing up her barnyard analogies. Perhaps you don't know as much as you think you do, Miss Tremaine. It's *swine* and pearls.'

She knew his condescension was deliberate but she couldn't help responding to the provocation. 'We didn't keep pigs. I had to come to Auckland to encounter the behaviour of common swine.'

'Er... hadn't we better be going now, Anne?' Rachel said hastily, picking up her leather satchel and getting to her feet, tugging her friend up with her.

'Anne?' The black eyebrows flattened. 'I thought your name was Katlin.'

It had had to happen and Anne was proud of the way she handled it, letting none of her trepidation show.

'My family calls me Anne,' she said with perfect truth. 'With an "e",' she added helpfully.

'Why?'

He wasn't asking about the 'e'.

'Because it's one of my names,' she said evasively. 'A lot of people don't like their middle names,' she said, choosing her random comments carefully to avoid an outright lie. 'I happen to like Anne. It's a good, plain, uncomplicated name.'

Now that *was* a lie. She had always wanted to be called something more dramatic. Alexandra or Laurel...or even Elizabeth would have done. A name you could do something *with* ...

His eyebrows rose again and she knew that he was thinking exactly what *she* was—that a plain, uncomplicated name suited her looks. Though her eyes were large and thickly lashed they were an indeterminate colour—sometimes hazel, sometimes muddy blue, more often hovering disappointingly somewhere in between. She might have just scraped by as pretty with her winged brows balanced by a nicely shaped mouth, except that in between was the noble Tremaine nose which threw her small face all out of kilter. Her brothers used to tease her that it was lucky she had also inherited the impressive Tremaine chest when she went through puberty, otherwise her centre of gravity wouldn't have shifted south of her chin!

Another impressive attribute, one that her brothers *never* teased her about because it had proved so vital to the family's well-being, was her unshakeable, unbreakable loyalty towards those she loved.

The car accident that had severely injured her mother's back when Anne was fifteen had been the start of the long process that had shaped her adult personality into that of a deeply compassionate woman, always willing to help those less fortunate than herself. Katlin had always been hopeless on the domestic front and at the time of the accident had already embarked on her obsession with writing, so it had naturally fallen to Anne to put aside her quiet dreams of university study and travel and buckle down to the task of being 'little mother' to the rest of the family. She had done it as she did most things, with a good-natured enthusiasm that had served to reassure her father and brothers, and especially her bed-ridden mother, that it was no great self-sacrifice for her to leave school without even minimum qualifications. In between the cooking and cleaning and caring for her mother Anne had plugged away at correspondence courses, which had gone some way to appeasing her hunger for knowledge and intellectual stimulation, and if occasionally she felt sorry for herself she never let it show.

Over the years she had maintained an attitude of obstinate optimism towards her mother's condition while everyone around her was losing hope. It had been a long, slow haul, but after numerous operations and continuing physical therapy Peg Tremaine's condition had gradually improved to the point where, although she still wasn't pain-free, she could move about and perform most household tasks without help. At last Anne had felt free to reclaim some of her childhood dreams, to fly the family nest and seek her own destiny.

But that destiny had immediately become inextricably bound up with Katlin's. Typically, Anne had found the bonds of love were too strong for her selfishly to ignore her sister's cry for help. So here she was, plain Anne masquerading as complex Katlin and shamefully beginning to enjoy it.

She frowned, daring him to take advantage of the opportunity for a fresh insult. It struck her that she had never frowned so much as she did in Hunter Lewis's company. It must be infectious.

'Anne was my grandmother's name,' Hunter Lewis said unexpectedly, a taunting amusement lightening his expression as he watched Rachel try a second time to edge her fierce little friend away.

'I suppose you're going to tell me she was tough as old boots and as mad as a snake,' said Anne darkly, shrugging off the tug at her elbow.

'Actually she was a darling, a sweet little lady with a heart as soft as butter.'

Anne waited warily for the punch line but it didn't come.

'Yes, well, I'm sure any grandmother of yours wouldn't dare be anything else,' she told him stubbornly. The expression in his eyes was masked as he glanced down at his watch and she added sarcastically, 'Oh, please, don't let us keep you. I'm sure there must be other people who actually have appointments to be intimidated by you.'

She was faintly appalled at the way she was carrying on but he merely gave her a sardonic smile. 'Are you saying I intimidate you, Anne?'

She had to tip her head back a long way to look him boldly in the eye. 'No.'

'I didn't think so,' he said drily. 'Then you won't be upset if I tell you that next time you leave anything behind in the washing machine I'm going to put it through the office shredder. Thanks to your carelessness I now have three pink shirts.'

Her red T-shirt! Anne put a hand over her mouth to stem a sudden giggle. She had wondered where it had gone after the last wash. Because it was a cheap one the unreliable dye meant it had to be separately washed in cold water and she had thrown it into the machine after having done Ivan's nappies on a hot cycle and scurried back to her loft to hang the nappies on a makeshift drying frame she had rigged up in front of her window. They took longer to dry than they would have flapping on the clothes-line outside the rooftop laundry-room but Anne couldn't risk using that any more than she dared leave them in the glass-fronted dryer.

'Perhaps you can use them to soften your image,' she said in a stifled voice.

'And perhaps I can just bill you for three new shirts.'

'And pigs might fly,' scoffed Anne with the insouci-ance of one who knew there was no blood in a stone.

'You were right.' He paused for Anne's puzzlement to register before he added smoothly, 'Your ignorance of porcine behaviour is evidently woefully complete.'

'*Porcine* behaviour?' Anne began to giggle again. 'Your pomposity is showing, Professor. You seem to have quite an interest in piggy—sorry, *porcine* activities. Is it a particular hobby of yours? What is it exactly that you're professor of anyway? Oh, that's right—piglitical studies...'

She went off into gales of irresistible laughter and Rachel began to laugh too, after first making sure that the volatile Professor Lewis wasn't going to explode on the spot. Instead he chose to leave, with a succinct comment about the declining standards of under-graduate humour.

'God, I thought you were begging him to blow his top, but you do know each other from somewhere, don't you?' giggled Rachel. 'You're not . . . ? Well, he made it sort of sound as if you were . . . well . . .'

'Living together? We are—sort of.' Anne gave a heavily edited version of her rent-free accommodation arrangements, only vaguely referring to a grant. Then she hastened to impress on her friend the need for discretion.

'If he asks you anything about me, don't tell him. *Especially* don't mention Ivan.'

'He doesn't know you have a baby next door?' Rachel was astonished. 'Does it negate the terms of your grant or something? I know I made Hunter sound a bit like Attila the Hun but he's not actually on permanent staff here, just holding a visiting lectureship, so it's not as if he was part of the stuffy university hierarchy or anything . . .'

'I'm not really sure,' said Anne, uncertainly answering all questions simultaneously. She hadn't read the fine print of the grant but presumed it was probably legal and binding. All she really had to go on was what Katlin had told her and Katlin wasn't exactly noted for her strict attention to detail.

'Just . . . be careful what you say, that's all. Not that I expect he'll be interested enough to ask,' she added hurriedly, seeing the speculation twinkling in Rachel's laughing eyes.

Later that afternoon, struggling up the stairs with Ivan in his push-chair, she rather regretted the pride that had made her refuse Rachel's standing offer of a lift to the nearest supermarket. She had caught the bus and on the way back it had rained, and although she had a plastic rain-shield on Ivan's push-chair she had had no cover for herself or the paper shopping bags on the uphill walk from the bus station.

She used her back to open the self-closing door beside the parking bay that led to the stairs, struggling to hook

the laden push-chair up the concrete step after her. Inside
the tiny bottom landing she paused to check the letterbox and stuff a letter into her damp pocket before
unloading the two soggy shopping bags from the wire
tray on top of the push-chair and placing them at the
bottom of the stairs. After a quick check up the stairwell
she picked up the push-chair containing Ivan and began
to hurry up the stairs. She had found it easier to carry
them both together than to take Ivan out and fold up
the push-chair and then juggle them both, the folded
push-chair being an unwieldy length for one of her
height, invariably banging painfully against her ankles
or trying to trip her up.

'Lucky for you, my fine fat friend, that I spent all
that time sheep-chasing otherwise I wouldn't be able to
manage this,' she panted at the second landing.

Ivan's dark eyes almost disappeared into his chubby
cheeks as he favoured her with his peculiar, slit-eyed grin
and sucked mightily at his fingers.

'Oh, yes, I know you're hungry. Aren't you always?
Well, you'll just have to wait until I can go back down
and get the food. I only have one pair of hands, you
know. A pity we can't ask the bad-tempered professor
to help, isn't it? I saw him today, and do you know what
he had the gall to say...?'

She told him all about it as she unlocked the loft and
carried him in, colouring the encounter by describing
how she had felt and what she had wanted to do rather
than what she actually had done. Ivan was a dream
listener. He never interrupted her or tried to contradict
her. His innocent baby ears were her diary into which
she described her days. It eased her occasional attacks
of loneliness and homesickness to have someone to
chatter to. She just hoped babies didn't have total recall.
She wouldn't like to think that in twenty years' time Ivan
would throw it all back at her.

She took him out of the push-chair and strapped him into his slanting baby-bouncer to keep him safe while she raced down to get the supermarket bags.

She was trying to cut down her shopping trips as much as possible but she was limited by the amount that she could carry at any one time.

Hugging a limp paper sack under each arm, she slogged back up the stairs, going ever faster as she felt the paper fibres beginning to collapse.

When she reached the last landing she stopped to re-adjust her cargo and suddenly became aware of a swift, almost noiseless step behind her. She whirled around, just in time for the man hurrying up the stairs behind her to cannon straight into her burdened arms.

Anne let out a soft shriek as she felt one of the soggy sacks split completely and watched in horror as a cascade of groceries poured down Hunter Lewis's chest. Fortunately they were all packaged goods and none broke open on impact, but Anne heard him swear under his breath as several cans bounced off his shoes.

There was a small silence punctuated by a staccato series of fading thumps as a can of baked beans rolled away down the stairs. Then Anne felt the bottom of the other bag begin to give and automatically clutched it tighter, one hand cupping the disintegrating packages at the same moment that Hunter reached forward with an impatient growl.

'Allow me——'

'No!' Remembering the packet of disposable nappies resting just below the serrated rim of paper, Anne jerked the bag sideways, out of his reach, and the carton of eggs which was lying on top of the nappies tilted and slid off the slippery surface of plastic wrapping, the lid flying open and three of the eggs catapulting through the air to smash against Hunter's chest.

'Oh, no!'

They both watched the broken yolks bleed into the slimy whites and drip down Hunter's tie. It was silk, by the look of it, pale blue with no pattern to hide the critical damage. His shirt had been cream.

'Why am I not surprised?' he rasped wearily.

'Well, I guess that's the price you pay for helping the environment,' Anne said weakly, raising her eyes to meet his smouldering gaze. 'The supermarket uses recycled paper bags rather than plastic—kinder to the environment but not as rainproof!'

'Which environment? It's obviously not mine,' he bit out. 'That makes it *four* shirts, I believe.'

'Don't be ridiculous,' she said hurriedly, envisaging her budget for the whole term going into his wardrobe. 'That one will be right as rain if it's washed straight away. It's only egg!'

'And the tie?'

'I suppose I could pay to have it dry-cleaned,' she said with a sigh, hoping he would gallantly refuse.

'I'd like it back by Friday.'

She scowled at his black head as he bent down to pick up the fallen groceries. 'If you'll open your door I'll put these in your kitchen.'

He wanted to go into her flat? Her eyes widened in dismay. 'No! I mean, you just collect the things up. I'll nip in and get a carton to put them in.'

She didn't given him a chance to reply. She delivered his orders and turned tail, dropping several more packets in her wake as she scrambled up the last few stairs and jiggled her key in the lock. She shut and bolted the door behind her before dumping her burden on the kitchen counter. The nappy pack was virtually the only thing that hadn't fallen out.

She grabbed one of the empty boxes left over from her move, making a quick, soothing sound to Ivan as she shot by him, and went through the same routine with

the front door in reverse, making sure it was securely
fastened before she joined Hunter Lewis on his haunches
beside the neat stack of her goods.

'If you give me your shirt I'll wash it for you and get
it back to you tomorrow,' she offered awkwardly.

'Thank you, but my wardrobe is depleted enough
already. I'll wash it myself by hand,' he said, his hand
pointedly brushing aside the thick braid that was leaking
rainwater on to the contents of the open carton.

'Suit yourself!' Anne snapped, flicking the wet braid
over her back.

'I usually do.'

'Why am I not surprised?' she murmured, parodying
his ironic first comment.

He didn't answer, studying the side of a box of baby-
rice with raised eyebrows. Uh-oh.

'I happen to like it, OK?' Anne snatched it out of his
hand and stuffed it into the carton. 'Do you have a
problem with that?'

'No. But I think you might. You must be even younger
than you look,' he said drily.

'Just because I'm not impossibly cynical and trying
to make everyone around me miserable, it doesn't mean
I'm a babe in arms!' she said hotly.

'So I see,' he murmured, eyeing the formerly demure
white shirt that was plastered by rain to her generous
breasts. 'Is that little homily supposed to be a jab at
me?'

'If the shoe fits!'

'For a promising writer you have a very hackneyed
turn of phrase.'

'That's because I save all the good stuff for my books,'
she told him tartly.

'The good stuff?' he echoed, his hard mouth kinking
in mocking amusement. 'Inelegant but succinct.'

'Thank you for that critique, Professor,' Anne said sarcastically as she straightened, grateful to have the heavy carton to hug to her chest. The way he had looked at her breasts had made her tingle uncomfortably.

'Let me carry that for you.'

'Thank you, but I'm quite capable,' she said, starting up the few remaining steps.

'At least give me your key so that you don't have to put that down to open your door.'

'I can manage,' she told him, stopping at the top and waiting for him to move on.

He studied her stubborn expression. A muscle moved in his bluntly square jaw as he said through his teeth, 'You really are the most incredibly...*irritating* woman...'

At least she had finally graduated to adulthood in his eyes! She grinned.

'Oh, I can be a lot more irritating than this,' she told him cheerfully. 'See you later, Professor!'

'Not if I see you first,' he delighted her by growling with childish petulance as he stumped off in the direction of his own door. 'And stop calling me Professor.'

'Why? Does it make you feel your age?' She wasn't going to let him have the last word.

'I'm only thirty-seven,' he shot back, ramming his key into the deadlock that adorned the battered entrance to his flat.

'Really?' she said wickedly, squinting at him along the length of the hall. 'You look much older. Maybe it's just because you're so surly——'

'I am not surly!'

He was yelling. Anne beamed at him. 'Don't burst a boiler, Prof. I'm sure you're utterly charming when you're with people of your own generation...'

She was giggling as she bolted him out. It was rather risky of her to taunt him but she just couldn't seem to help it. Something about him just seemed to beg her for a provoking response. She had never known a man whose emotions simmered so close to the surface. Her father and brothers were real men of the land who had an earthy sense of humour and were stoically good-natured. Anne could tease and provoke them and they would only laugh and brush her off like a pesky fly.

Hunter Lewis was definitely outside her experience and, as Anne wistfully informed Ivan over his puréed vegetables, experience was one of the things she had come to Auckland to obtain!

CHAPTER THREE

ANNE took a big breath before knocking on the door, her nervousness making her fist land a little harder than she had intended. She took another deep, unsteady breath as the door began to open and then nearly fell over at the sight of Hunter Lewis in a towel.

Much as she hated to admit it, he was very impressive, the bulky, well-defined muscles flowing over his shoulders into a deep chest, the sculpted power of which was evident even through the masking of dense, dark hair. He was certainly every inch a man, she thought as her eyes helplessly traced the inverted triangle of hair that tapered from a broad hand span between his masculine nipples to an enticing narrow line that dipped beneath the white towel insecurely hitched around lean hips. His belly was as taut and tanned as the rest of him and his long legs were strong and sinewy, smothered with the same silky-rough black hair that covered his chest. Patches of water glistened on his bare skin and glinted in his body hair, as if he had been interrupted in the process of drying himself.

'Seen enough?'

She wondered wickedly what he would do if she said no. Hurriedly she tore her gaze away from the taut pull of towelling across his flanks and summoned all her meagre acting powers. She edged closer.

'Uh, I made some pasta sauce and I thought you might like some...as a kind of thank-you—for helping me with my shopping the other day. And I have your tie here too, all cleaned and pressed.' He had said he had wanted it by Friday and she hoped she would get Brownie points for delivering it a day early although his expression wasn't encouraging.

She gave him a coolly restrained smile that she hoped was unthreatening and lifted the covered plastic container in one hand, offering his tie with the other. She had no intention of telling him that she had carefully washed and pressed it herself in clear defiance of its bossy care-tag. At the moment a dry-cleaning bill was effectively as far beyond her budget as a new silk tie would have been, so she'd figured she had nothing to lose.

He reached for the tie but made no attempt to accept the pasta sauce, and she took advantage of his sudden need to anchor his slipping towel and ducked under his arm to saunter into his flat.

'Come in, why don't you?' he murmured ironically, turning to follow her.

'Thanks, I will...just for a moment,' she said cheerfully, as if he had uttered a gushing welcome and she was merely being polite.

The physical layout of his loft, she discovered to her intense interest, was virtually a mirror-image of her own, but there any resemblance ended. Here lived sinful luxury instead of artful practicality.

There was oatmeal carpet underfoot, so thick and soft that her sandalled feet sank down into it, and the walls were colour-washed a pale terracotta, dappled with either sponge or brush to produce a stippled effect that provided an interesting background for the gilt-framed paintings which lined the walls. Floor-to-ceiling wooden bookcases surrounded the familiar high, arched windows at one end and at the other was a huge, ornately gold-framed mirror that took up almost the whole of the wall that backed on to her flat, effectively doubling the apparent length of the room, the reflection of the sky making it seem lighter and airier even now, with rain pouring down outside and dusk approaching. The dancer in Anne coveted that mirror immediately, while the lazy hedonist in her lusted after the butter-soft apricot leather of the squatly over-sized couch and chairs.

His kitchen was larger than hers, cleverly designed to encompass the leading edge of culinary technology, and as she put the plastic tub down on the marble bench Anne had the uneasy feeling that her economical but tasty recipe for pasta sauce might be somewhat out of its element. Rather as she was in her swirling home-made skirt and loose peasant blouse. Then her glance fell on the reason for her generosity and damped down her qualms.

'All you have to do is heat this for...' As she turned back from her spying mission she discovered that her instructions were being delivered to empty air. Hunter Lewis had disappeared with the same uncanny quietness with which he was prone to appear. She looked at the telephone on the kitchen wall and wondered if she dared take advantage of his absence, but decided that it would be unwise to antagonise him further than she already had. It was a major achievement just to have got inside his flat.

She moved to take a closer look at some of his paintings. Originals, of course—prints were probably beneath his dignity, she thought wryly—but his selection was an eclectic mix which suggested that they were chosen with the heart and eye rather than the dictates of an investment portfolio.

'Don't you like it?'

She jumped as Hunter materialised in the doorway beside the painting which she was studying with a frown. His bedroom, she surmised, and realised with a small hitch of her breathing that his cotton crew-necked shirt and unbleached linen trousers didn't quite blot out the mental image of him in a towel.

She looked at the painting again. 'No,' she said bluntly, before she remembered that she was supposed to be buttering him up and began hurriedly back-tracking. 'Th-that is, I don't really know much about art so I really can't——'

'I didn't ask for artistic criticism. I asked whether you liked it.'

'Does it matter?' she hedged, wondering belatedly whether he might have painted it himself. She tried to squint at the signature without being too obvious.

'No, it isn't mine. I have no skill with a paintbrush whatsoever. So you're not going to be insulting my talent by telling me you don't like my taste in art...nor, I hope, my intelligence with polite lies,' he added silkily as she nibbled at her lower lip.

'All right, I loathe it,' she was neatly trapped into admitting sullenly. 'I can't make head or tail of it and I don't like the colours. Satisfied?' Her eyebrows almost flew off her face as she regarded him haughtily.

'Completely. Actually, it was painted by my mother.'

Anne closed her eyes. When she opened them again gold flecks were smouldering in the blue irises at the discovery that he was laughing at her. 'My commiserations to your father,' she said insultingly.

'My parents were divorced when I was still at primary school. My father's dead now, but he shared your dislike of my mother's art.'

Anne gave up and allowed the vivid blush of remorse that had been lurking under her temper to swallow her up.

'I'm sorry,' she mumbled. Why did her good intentions towards this man always go up in smoke? 'I'm sure your mother is a very good artist——'

'The international art world seems to think so,' Hunter interrupted blandly. 'She's very well-known. In fact, I had to pay several thousand dollars for that painting that you find so unlikeable.'

Anne was instantly outraged on his behalf. 'She made you *pay* for one of her paintings? Her own *son*?'

'Only indirectly. I bought it retail from a gallery. My mother often gives me a painting for my birthday or for Christmas. But when I asked for this particular one she refused—sold it outright to the gallery instead...'

'Why?'

Anne knew all about artistic temperament. It was prone to flights of illogic that could verge on the ridiculous—which she and Ivan could thank for their current sojourn in the city. In Katlin's view the artistic ends justified the means. It was left to Anne to endure the pangs of conscience suffered by less talented mortals.

She had smothered her deepest doubts about what they were doing by insisting on an absolute minimum of outright lying, enrolling at the university under her own name and simply saying, 'Call me Anne,' whenever someone addressed her as Katlin. It usually worked— they accepted the correction politely, without question...except for this man, of course.

But it was tough. Not least because she still worried about whether she was doing the right thing for Katlin and Ivan in the long term.

Anne herself could never envisage a situation where she would put her career ahead of the needs of her own baby, but neither could she condemn Katlin for being different. Her pregnancy had been a very difficult one and mother and child had almost died during Ivan's premature birth.

Afterwards, when Katlin had taken the baby back to the tiny, isolated cabin on the coast that she called home, she had found to her horror that the words that had once flowed so easily from her pen had completely dried up. With another's needs taking precedence over her own she could no longer achieve the necessary physical and mental peace that she required for her writing. She had stubbornly resisted Anne's pleas to contact the baby's father.

Anne, who had stayed with her sister to help her through the first month of solo parenthood, had been alarmed on later visits by her sister's deepening listlessness. She had been thrilled when the recipient of this year's Markham Grant had been finally announced, thinking that it might be just what Katlin needed to bounce her out of her slough of despond.

It had, but not in the way that Anne had fondly envisaged. She had been a great deal less thrilled with her sister's brilliant solution to the problem of her ongoing writer's block but, after discreetly consulting Katlin's doctor about his concerns for his patient's mental and physical health, she had reluctantly allowed herself to be persuaded.

Hunter was regarding her morose expression thoughtfully. 'My mother doesn't like this painting either. She regards it as a depressing aberration in her abstract style.'

Anne perked up at the realisation that her *faux pas* hadn't been quite so bad after all. 'Then why did you buy it?'

His square-cut mouth pulled into a mocking curve. 'To annoy her. She lives in a rarefied environment of more or less undiluted praise these days. She sometimes needs reminding that she's as human as the rest of us.'

'A very expensive way to make your point,' said Anne disapprovingly, thinking that Hunter Lewis evidently didn't have to struggle along on a mere lecturer's income, to be able to indulge such an expensive whim. 'And not very filial either.'

'Do I take it you believe that family loyalty should override other ethical considerations . . . like personal integrity or honesty, or expecting people to accept responsibility for their own actions?'

Anne's eyes skated away from his. He was speaking idly and at random, she reminded herself. 'Blood *is* thicker than water,' she muttered uneasily.

'Ah, yes, I forgot you have a cliché for every occasion. So you believe that the rights of the individual are paramount over the rights of the state?'

'I didn't come here for a political discussion,' she said gruffly, feeling guiltier than ever before.

'No, that's right.' He strolled over to the kitchen and lifted the lid off her pasta sauce, giving her a cynical smile as he bent to inhale the smell of the contents. 'You came to deliver the poor bachelor a wholesome, home-cooked meal—purely out of the goodness of your heart... A bit heavy-handed with the dried basil, weren't you?'

'I'll have you know I only use fresh herbs when I cook and there's *exactly* the right amount of basil in there,' Anne said, infuriated by his casual criticism. 'I've made that sauce hundreds of times and no one's ever complained before...'

'Perhaps country palates aren't as discriminating as city-bred ones——'

Anne said a rude word, then blushed when his eyebrows rose.

'What makes you such an expert anyway?' she said defensively.

'I was taught classic cuisine by an Italian chef.'

Anne resisted the urge to snatch back her modest offering. 'You took a cooking course?'

'Not as such. Maria gave me lessons purely out of the goodness of her heart.'

Irony threaded the innocent statement and the wicked glint of anticipation in his black eyes warned Anne not to make the obvious mistake of enquiring further into

Maria's identity. She had a feeling that he would enjoy embarrassing her by telling her that it was not only as a chef that the woman had excelled.

'Naturally you don't have to eat it if it's not up to your impeccable standard,' she said stiffly.

'No doubt I'll manage to choke it down.'

She felt a very strong desire to empty the sauce over his supercilious head. The amount of best-quality beef mince that she had used in the sauce would have lasted her three meals.

'Oh, please, don't suffer on my account,' she snapped.

'I won't,' he assured her smoothly, and there was a small silence.

She sighed. It would appear that she was going to have to grovel after all, since her bribery had patently failed to charm. She caught her plait over her shoulder and began fiddling with the end as the silence lengthened.

'By the way, while you're here . . .'

'Yes?' She brightened, her eyes shifting from gloomy hazel to hopeful blue at his apparent tentativeness. Perhaps he wanted to ask a small favour of *her*, thereby enabling her casually to suggest a trade!

'Perhaps you'd like to use my telephone?'

'Telephone?' she echoed blankly, hoping her shock would be mistaken for polite surprise.

'That *is* why you're here, isn't it?' His voice was a strange mixture of gravel and silk.

'Whatever makes you say that?' she said bravely.

'The way you keep sneaking glances at it. The phone box down the street has been vandalised, I noticed yesterday. And now here you are, oozing charm to a surly brute——'

'I never called you a brute!' she protested weakly. 'A brute is unreasoning and unintelligent——'

'You must think me both if you expected to fool me so easily, after making such a point of avoiding me like the plague since you moved in——'

'Since you've so kindly and unexpectedly *offered*, I may as well take advantage of your good temper,' interrupted Anne loftily. She marched over to the wall and lifted up the receiver. 'You know, you're a very mistrustful man,' she said as she dialled the number. 'If you remember it was *your* not so subtle suggestion that we avoid each other.'

'I didn't expect you to take me quite so literally.'

'No, you expected me to fling myself at you——'

'Or to start knocking at my door every five minutes, sweetly offering me home-cooked meals and asking to use the phone,' he interposed pointedly.

She glared at him and turned her back as the telephone was answered.

'Rachel?' Conscious of her audience, she hurried to make her call as short as possible. 'My morning tutorial has been cancelled for tomorrow so I'm not going to be coming in. Do you want to drop by here after your lecture so we can go over that Russian test, or do you want to leave it until the weekend?'

She turned again as Hunter brushed past her to move about the kitchen. As she listened to Rachel run through her crammed weekend social schedule she watched him out of the corner of her eye, noting how thoroughly comfortable he was in his surroundings. She saw him take a pot from a drawer beneath the ceramic cook-top and empty the contents of her square plastic container into it. Instead of scraping it with a spoon as she would have done, he hooked a bottle of red wine out of the rack built into the wall above her head and deftly opened it, rinsing the remains of the sauce out of the corners of the container with a hefty slug.

She forced her attention back to the voice in her ear. 'Uh...no, thanks...really, I just have too much work to do... I've got a few assignments going already...and a lot of writing to do,' she added hurriedly for the benefit of the man untangling what looked like freshly made fettucine on the marble bench-top. 'Oh, sure, maybe another time...' Much as she liked Rachel, the night-clubbing social life that her friend enjoyed was not for her. Unlike Rachel, Anne couldn't afford to fail any of her papers so most of her spare time had to be dedicated to studying, or earning some extra income. 'OK. I'll see you Sunday evening, then. Bye!'

She hung up. 'Thanks.'

He didn't turn around, concentrating on coiling up the ribbons of pasta. 'I know I should say, Any time, but we both know that would be a polite lie.'

'This was sort of an emergency,' she explained.

'So I heard. I get the feeling that there are going to be a lot of sort-of-an-emergencies in your life, so perhaps we'd better define a set time convenient to both of us that you can use the telephone.'

Anne opened her mouth to refuse haughtily, and realised that pride was getting in the way of good sense. 'Well...'

He made it easy for her. 'How about not before six or after seven?'

She was usually up well before six at home but her metabolism was already adjusting to lazy city ways. 'Uh, I think that might be a bit early...'

He turned his head, his look wry. 'I meant in the evenings, Anne. I like a lie-in in the mornings myself.'

She could imagine it. That big, bronze body sprawled across white sheets. Since he didn't have any bodily imperfections to hide he probably slept in the raw...and within touching distance of Anne if there hadn't been a wall between them. She knew his bed was hard up against the same wall as hers because sometimes, when she woke up at night, she could hear the protest of his bedsprings as he turned over.

'Anne?'

'Mmm? Oh, sure. But I don't expect it will be very often. I'm sure they'll fix the phone down the road soon.'

'When they do, make sure you make your calls during daylight hours. It's not a good idea for a lone female to stand in a lighted phone booth by herself at night, even in this part of town.'

Anne's feminist instincts bristled. 'I can look after myself, thank you.'

'It doesn't look like it. You're fairly small——'

She knew he wasn't complimenting her on her slenderness. 'I'm compact,' she corrected him. 'I keep very fit, as you must know from all the thumping you do on my wall. And I have four brothers back at home!' She announced the fact as if it explained everything.

Evidently it didn't to him—a dead give-away that he was an only child. 'They're not going to do you much good there,' he scoffed.

'I didn't mean I need them to *defend* me. I meant that growing up with them taught me how to fight dirty. I broke Rex's arm once, and he's taller than you!'

She hooked her thumbs into the waistband of her skirt in a boastful stance that threw out her chest.

'What did you do, batter him to the ground with your br-braids?'

She eyed him suspiciously but he didn't react. Perhaps she had misjudged that small stammer.

'Actually I fell on him,' she admitted reluctantly. 'Out of a tree. He was trying to shake me down, so I came down. Knocked him flat. He was sixteen at the time and he howled like a baby.' The smile she gave him was redolent of bloodthirsty pleasure.

'How old were you?'

'Thirteen . . .'

She bit her lip. She had forgotten that, as Katlin, she was supposed to be the eldest. Thank goodness she hadn't given the childhood encounter any time reference. Hunter had no way of knowing how old the real winner of the Markham Grant was but she shouldn't have taken the risk. Anne knew that she didn't look her own twenty-three years, let alone Katlin's twenty-eight.

She bent over and peered into the pot he had set on the cook-top, giving her sauce an brisk stir with the wooden spoon he had left resting across the top.

'Wouldn't this have been quicker in the microwave?' she offered helpfully.

'Quicker but not better,' he said, accepting the change of subject as he filled a large pot with cold water and set it on another ring, flicking one of the dials inset into the bench on to high. 'A long, slow blending of flavours always results in a better dish than a brief jostle of molecules. I want to give the wine time to mature the flavour.'

'I suppose you think that only culinary philistines use microwaves,' she sighed. Naturally someone like Hunter Lewis wouldn't have to take the reduced power costs of using a microwave into his equation!

'Not at all. They have their uses. I take it you like pasta?'

She looked at him, in his casually elegant clothes, in his casually elegant kitchen. 'It's cheap, tasty and nutritious . . . What's not to like?'

He rinsed his hands in the sink and turned to rest a solid hip against the marble counter as he dried his hands on a linen tea-towel and studied her mobile expression.

'Do you resent me for what I have, Anne?' he drawled with uncanny perception. 'Is that where all this subtle hostility of yours is aimed? I assure you, most of what I have I've worked hard to earn for myself.'

'I work hard too,' she shot back.

'Oh? When?'

'What do you mean, when?' Did he think she was a scrounger because she was supposedly living on a grant?

'When do you write?'

Anne nibbled her full lower lip. 'I'm writing all the time,' she said defensively.

'I don't doubt it. Russian, Japanese and anthropology, isn't it?' Anne's heart sank as she realised he must have looked her up in the university files. It might have been idle curiosity on his part, but what if he decided to dig further?

'I'm not talking about compiling course assignments,' he continued in a tone of voice which she thought he probably used on recalcitrant students—crisp and lightly sarcastic. 'I'm talking about *writing*. That *is* why you're here, isn't it—to finish a first novel for publication? If you're taking on a heavy study-load, when are you going to find the necessary writing time for yourself? And don't tell me you can fit it in here and there . . . creative writing involves a sustained, concentrated effort——'

'I write best at night,' protested Anne, hating him for trapping her into another lie.

'All the more reason to take it easy during the day,' Hunter pointed out, his shrewd, black-eyed gaze steady as he returned to the main attack. 'Exactly when at night? I stay up pretty late myself and I haven't heard your typewriter pounding away very often.'

'I like to revise my work by hand,' she said quickly. If he could hear her typewriter from her living-room, then the walls were even thinner than she had realised.

'You must be doing an awful lot of editing compared to the amount you're writing,' he commented thoughtfully.

'Uh, well, I haven't really settled to a routine yet . . .'

'After several weeks? In my experience writers usually have to have their regular creative fix or go crazy. Have you set yourself goals? Or are you suffering from writer's block?'

'I guess, in a way,' Anne said wryly. 'I'm just going through a period of adjustment——'

'Then probably the worst thing you could do is to stop, or load yourself up with other distractions!'

She might have known that his sympathy would be backed with infuriating logic. 'Thank you for your advice but I'm sure everything will sort itself out,' she said firmly, hoping that Katlin was justifying her confidence by writing her head off in her isolated little eyrie at Golden Bay.

'Translated: you're going to ignore the problem and hope it goes away of its own accord.' His disapproval was obvious. Anne didn't doubt that any difficulties he encountered he met head-up and head-on.

'*One* of my problems, anyway,' Anne said meaningfully. 'I suppose it's an occupational hazard of being a professor—this constant urge to lecture people. I thought politics, not literature, was your particular field of expertise.'

'The whole essence of politics is human behaviour—the complex of relationships that people form to empower their beliefs and invest themselves with authority over others. In its adjectival sense it was very *politic* of you to evade my original question . . . Do you resent me for what I have?'

'Not for what you have but for what you are,' Anne said flatly, glad to get off the subject of her non-existent novel.

'And what am I?'

'Don't tempt me,' she threatened.

His heavy lids drooped lazily. 'Oh, come on. You've been perfectly free with your insulting opinions of me so far. Why stop now?'

Is that what he thought? Not so devastatingly perceptive after all, thought Anne impishly. 'You're intelligent, strong, utterly independent and self-confident to the point of arrogance,' she frankly listed the personal assets she found so irritating.

He stared at her for a moment, his eyes narrowing with a faintly arrested intensity as he realised that she was perfectly serious. Then the square mouth tilted slowly in amusement. 'You forgot handsome.'

'That's because you're not,' she snapped.

'Then why did you look me over in my towel as if I were a *Cosmopolitan* centrefold?'

She could hardly deny it but she refused to blush at the remembered image of his semi-nudity, lifting her chin and answering baldly. 'Because you looked like one. You have a big, sexy body. That doesn't make you handsome. And it doesn't help that you frown too much. You'll probably have train-tracks across your forehead by the time you're forty,' she took pleasure in telling him.

'But I'll still have my big, sexy body,' he reminded her slyly. 'I'd rather have that than a pretty face.'

'Is that why you're not married?' she said, wilfully misunderstanding in order not to be in agreement with him. 'Do you live alone because you don't want a feminine face around, distracting you from your loving self-absorption?'

'Are you accusing me of being an onanist, Anne?' he asked blandly.

'I might...if I knew what it meant,' she confessed warily.

'Someone who actively enjoys sexual self-sufficiency,' he said obliquely, so that it was a moment before she fully comprehended his meaning.

'Oh. *Oh*!' She blushed vividly under his glittering black gaze and he laughed. His laugh, like his voice, was unexpectedly mellow for a man of his temperament and toughness. He was, she was beginning to realise to her dismay, a very much more attractive man than she had at first suspected.

'So you were wrong about my being *utterly* independent,' he pointed out, turning his attention back to the bench. 'There are certain things that I still have to depend on others to provide for me. And I *was* married . . . once. How much fettucine would you like?'

'I beg your pardon?' she murmured, still trying to conquer her embarrassment, and her curiosity over that casual mention of his marriage. And his phrasing was intriguing—'still have to depend'—as if the most intimate form of human interaction was something he looked upon as a tiresome, practical physical necessity rather than a deeply desirable, emotionally fulfilling experience.

'I can hardly eat all this myself.'

'Are you asking me to have dinner with you?' she asked, startled by the notion.

'That's what you expected me to do, isn't it?' he asked drily. 'When I discovered there was more than enough here for two . . .'

'No, it's not what I expected!' she erupted, annoyed at the implication. 'I just thought your appetite would match your size, that's all. I certainly don't need to resort to underhanded tactics to get dinner dates——'

'Do I take it you're refusing my kind invitation?' he murmured, looking undismayed by her rejection and confirming her belief that he had been merely goading her.

In the brief silence in which she searched for a sufficiently crushing reply there came a sudden, high-pitched and very distinctive sound from the other side of the apartment. Hunter's black head snapped around to focus on the noise and Anne tensed, coughing loudly and making a great show of looking at her watch.

'Gosh, look at the time! Well, thanks for the phone; I really must rush—I've got my own dinner on...' She started backing towards the door, still making distracting rumbling sounds in her throat. Hunter rotated slowly back to face her.

'What was that?'

'What?'

He tipped his head back and, as if on cue, the sound came again and this time no amount of coughing was going to disguise that it was coming from her flat on the other side of the wall.

'Maybe I left my radio on,' Anne improvised hopefully, and stitched on a brilliant smile just as the sound intensified into an angry wail. Oh, no, not now, Ivan. Please, of all times, not *now*... Anne began to pray silently as she progressed blindly in what she hoped was the right direction, trying to keep a nonchalant expression on her face.

'That's not music. Not even what *you* claim passes for music.' Hunter prowled around the counter towards her, his black eyes brooding with a growing suspicion as she skittered backwards. 'It sounds much more like a——'

'Cat! Yes, you're right, it's probably a cat.' She tried to force the words into his grim mouth. 'There are quite a few strays yowling around the warehouse, I notice,' she gabbled as she scrabbled behind her for the doorhandle, aware of the wail starting to subside into a series of hiccuping sobs that were all too human. 'The men must feed them their lunch scraps. They can get up the fire-escape, you know—the cats, that is, not the men. I left the window open... Maybe one got in and got trapped. Oh, look, your pasta water's boiling. You stay and cook your meal. I'll just——'

Her words were cut off as thoroughly as her escape as Hunter's big frame blocked the doorway.

'If that's a cat then I'm a monkey's uncle,' he grated, pushing past her and heading towards her unlocked door.

Ten seconds later he was looming accusingly over Anne as she scooped a red-cheeked Ivan up from the cot and cradled him protectively to her breast.

'Yes, it's a baby! And no, he's not visiting. His name is Ivan Tremaine and he lives here with me. Stop glaring at us like that—you're frightening him!'

This despite the fact that as soon as Ivan had spotted the loud stranger he had halted in mid-cry and was now squinting at this new visual toy with every appearance of glee, the tear-stains on his feverish cheeks rapidly drying.

Anne felt like bursting into tears herself as she faced Hunter's searing disapproval, but she sensed it would gain her little sympathy. He had the fierce look of a man who wasn't going to budge without some very good answers.

She'd better think of some—fast!

CHAPTER FOUR

'ARE you telling me that you left a helpless baby alone in the flat?' Hunter's expression was one of grim disapproval.

Anne drew herself up defensively. So it was to be the easy questions first!

'Only for a few minutes. He was asleep when I left and I was only a few metres away, for goodness' sake! I heard him cry, didn't I?'

'Where did he come from?'

'The stork brought him, where do you think he came from?' she snapped, patting Ivan's nappy, automatically checking it for dampness.

Hunter's black brows descended even further over his hooded gaze as he observed the practised familiarity of her actions.

'You mean he's yours? You're his *mother*?' He sounded sharply incredulous and the next words were blurted out in an almost violent repudiation of the very concept. 'How in God's name did *that* happen?'

Anne hesitated on the brink of correcting his stupendous mistake. Then the memory of Katlin's impassioned pleas locked her hasty words in her throat.

She had faithfully promised her sister that she would look after Ivan until Katlin had finished her book or until the grant ran out, whichever was soonest. It could be as little as a few months or as long as a year. Another year of her life wasn't so much to ask, not when it came with a glittering bribe—the opportunity for Anne to do exactly what she had planned to do with her freedom anyway: live and study at the most prestigious university campus in the country.

Katlin's whole future, she had claimed, hinged on Anne's taking her place at the Auckland flat, because if the recipient of the Markham Grant didn't take up the offered residency then he or she forfeited both the income and—more importantly as far as Katlin was concerned—the associated publishing contract. To Katlin, now clinging to the conviction that Golden Bay was the mystical source of her inspiration and the only place she would be able to reproduce the powerful intensity of writing that had characterised the first three chapters of her book, Anne was the perfect solution.

To her secret chagrin, a cowardly part of Anne had actually welcomed the emotional blackmail that ensured she didn't have to venture out into the big, wide, unknown world *completely* alone. Ivan was a wonderful human security blanket, comforting her with the constant reminder that if her dreams failed her there was always family and home.

If she told Hunter that Ivan was only her nephew he would inevitably want to know more about her sister and Anne didn't trust herself not to get impossibly tangled up in lies. And if it became generally known that Katlin had a son...well, the foundation wasn't aware that she'd become a solo mother in the months between her posting them the first three chapters of her book for consideration and their awarding of the prize. Perhaps it wouldn't make any difference, but Katlin had refused to take the risk. 'Keep your head down and your mouth shut', had been her final anthem.

Anyway, Anne had probably been more of a mother to Ivan so far than Katlin and she even had an official maternal title, albeit only as godmother.

'Babies don't just *happen*,' she pointed out sarcastically to the impatiently waiting man. 'I would have thought that a man with a university education would have at least *some* idea of how babies are made——'

'I was speaking geographically and you damned well know it,' he growled.

Anne's pleasure in thwarting his curiosity was beginning to eclipse her guilty apprehension. 'Ivan was born near Nelson——' she began primly.

Hunter smothered an expletive. 'Where has he been until now?' he cut her off rudely. 'Who's been looking after him for you?'

'No one. He's been living here with me ever since I moved in,' she said with some relish. 'You just never noticed him before.'

His black brows tilted sharply as he contemplated the statement, obviously rerunning all of their previous encounters through his formidable brain. 'Because you made damned sure I didn't,' he realised slowly.

'Ivan is a naturally placid baby,' Anne replied calmly, and then flinched as Hunter suddenly reached out and pulled her left hand away from the baby's squirming back. She wrenched it free as she realised what he was doing—checking her finger for a non-existent ring. No doubt she was now being filed in his mind as careless or sexually irresponsible.

Sighing, Anne decided that there was no point in trying to settle Ivan down with a pit bull snapping and snarling about her for information. She murmured soothingly to her whimpering nephew as she swept back out into the long room, Hunter dogging her heels.

'You were hiding him,' he accused. 'Isn't that a bit Victorian? An illegitimate baby is hardly a reason for shame these days.'

She whirled on him, making Ivan gurgle at the sudden motion. 'I'm not ashamed of him!'

'Then why pretend you're living here alone?'

Before she could think of a suitably smoke-screened answer he found the logic of it himself.

'Good God, the Markham people don't know you have a baby, do they?'

She glared at him, feeling cornered.

'Do they, Anne?' he insisted.

She got the feeling that he would question her all night if she didn't answer. 'No,' she said sullenly, her mouth offering the suggestion of a defiant pout, her arms instinctively holding Ivan tighter until he coughed, a gentlemanly hint.

'You're holding him too tightly.'

She bristled at his critical tone. Was he going to accuse her of child abuse now? 'Don't tell me how to hold my...my...' She couldn't quite get the word out and kissed the silky top of Ivan's head instead, her fiercely protective love speaking the lie for her.

'Your son,' Hunter provided obligingly. His black eyes narrowed as he minutely inspected their faces. 'He doesn't look anything like you.'

Anne flushed guiltily. The family were agreed that Ivan had Katlin's nose and square face, but he certainly didn't have her blonde colouring or highly strung personality.

'Does he take after his father?'

'I...I suppose...I don't really know,' she floundered, wondering, not for the first time, whether if she had met Dmitri and explained a bit about her sister's background things would have turned out differently for Katlin. But in her love-affair, as in most aspects of her life, Katlin had been highly secretive, only admitting it when she could no longer hide her pregnancy.

'You don't know what he looks like?' He pounced on her uncertainty and naturally drew the most insulting deduction possible. 'Do you even know who the father is?'

Anne stiffened at the slur, angered on her sister's behalf. 'Of course I do! He was a sailor.'

'Was? You mean he's dead?'

'No. He's just...not around any more. He...he sailed off again with his ship,' she said vaguely. At least, she assumed that he had. Katlin had kept most of the details to herself.

'Is that all you know about him? That he was a sailor? What about his name? Do you at least know that?'

Anne felt her flush deepen, torn between fresh outrage and bubbling amusement.

Hunter was making her sound utterly amoral, which was laughable since her sexual experience was limited to a few back-seat tussles when she was fifteen. After her mother's accident she had had precious little time for the kind of freedom that Katlin and her older brothers had taken for granted during their teenage years.

'His name is Dmitri and he's Russian.' It was everything that she knew and she sought for a way to get him off the awkward subject of Ivan's conception. 'Look, Hunter——'

'Is that why you're studying Russian, because of Ivan's father?'

'No, of course not!' This time she was offended on her own behalf. 'I've always been interested in Russia and Russians——'

'Obviously,' he cut in, with a pointed look at Ivan, who was now starting to fuss in her arms.

'Not in *that* way. Shush, darling...'

'I beg your pardon?' he drawled mockingly.

'Not *you*...Ivan.' She couldn't imagine anyone daring to call Hunter Lewis darling. 'I think he must be getting another tooth...he's usually so good. I told you, he hardly ever cries...'

'Mmm. Let's have a look.'

To her shock Hunter bent over and stroked a strong masculine finger down Ivan's flushed cheek before slipping it into his fretful mouth, rubbing it firmly back and forth across his lower gums.

Ivan immediately grabbed at the thick, furry wrist and hung on with both hands, gnawing enthusiastically at the strange finger with his two upper teeth.

'Steady on there, Tiger... Mmm, definitely a cutting edge emerging among the bumps.' Hunter withdrew his finger and casually wiped off the sticky drool against his shirt with none of the distaste that Anne normally observed in males. However, she had no intention of allowing him to see that she was charmed.

'Thank you for the second opinion, Dr Spock.' Her voice was heavy with lofty sarcasm.

'Actually I am a doctor, but not of the medical variety,' he said meekly, amusement flickering across his hard face as she gave him a look which said she was supremely unimpressed with the information. She wasn't going to let on that she had looked up his scanty biographical details in the university staff information booklet as soon as she had discovered his identity.

'I suppose you're as much an expert on children as you are at cooking,' she said dismissively, hitching a wriggling Ivan higher on her hip. 'Have you got any of your own?'

'My wife couldn't have children,' he said, his amusement abruptly dying.

'Oh.'

Was that the reason that he was no longer married? She longed to pry but the coldness in the deep black eyes was warning enough. She looked down at Ivan, and imagined what it would be like to know that this was as close as she would ever get to holding a child of her own flesh. A hollow formed in her heart and was immediately filled with a sympathetic ache of loss.

'I've got some gel here somewhere . . . to rub on his gums,' she muttered, suppressing the surge of unwilling empathy.

'Why don't you go and find it? I'll hold the young chap.'

He reached for the squirming bundle and Anne stepped back, startled. 'That's OK, I——'

'You like to be independent, yes, I've gathered that. Very commendable of you, but there's no need to carry it to extremes. Give him to me.'

His hands were as firm as his tone as he slid them around the nappy-padded hips, and the small, undignified struggle for possession came to its natural conclusion when Anne felt the hard knuckles digging in and rubbing against her soft breasts. The friction made her nipples unexpectedly tingle and tighten and she hurriedly released her burden, hoping he hadn't noticed her body's small, betraying reaction.

Of course, he had. As he stepped away with Ivan his eyes flickered downwards and it took an effort of will not to wrap her arms protectively over her chest. He can't really see anything, she told herself. Although the elasticated neck of her white blouse was fairly low, it puffed out over her breasts and there was also her bra forming a second line of defence. Unfortunately his gaze proved to be as disturbing as his inadvertent touching and she could feel her breasts continue to tighten. It was a delicious, alien sensation that made her remember with uncomfortable vividness the splendour of his earlier seminudity.

His eyes rose again to hers and she was impaled by the blade-sharp curiosity she saw there, recognising it instinctively as sexual. She was suddenly acutely aware of the physical differences between them. Was this how he had felt when she had run her eyes over him? Heaven forbid!

'I'll just get that gel...' She spun away and rushed into the bathroom to fossick in the cabinet.

'Control yourself,' she scolded herself in the mirror as she found the small tube and snapped the cabinet closed. Her reflection looked shamefully hot and bothered. 'Or he's going to think you're promiscuous as well as irresponsible.'

'Don't tell me you're hiding someone else in there?'

She jumped at the sound of his amused voice, floating in through the open door.

'Just talking to myself,' she said as she briefly held a cold flannel to her cheeks before re-emerging from the bathroom, hopefully looking more serene. The serenity received a sharp nudge at the sight of Hunter and Ivan, so perfectly matched in colouring and sharp-eyed inquisitiveness as they watched her approach.

'Do you do that often?' he asked.

'Talk to myself? All the time. I have more interesting conversations that way,' she said, giving him a pointed look before turning her attention to Ivan.

'Open up, darling. This is going to make you feel so-o-o good. Oh, yes, isn't that nice...?' She rubbed the gel into his eager gums, alternately babbling encouragement and instructions for Hunter to hold still. 'Yes, that feels so good when I do that, doesn't it, darling...? Oh, yes, oh, yes, oh, yes...'

'You know, anyone eavesdropping on this conversation might get the wrong idea about what's going on,' murmured Hunter drily.

'Hmm?' Her incomprehension lasted only the few seconds it took to register the wicked smirk behind his bland expression. 'I doubt it, not if they knew you were in here. You're nearly forty after all,' she said witheringly, remembering his knee-jerk reaction to her last taunts about his age.

'If I recall rightly, you're not all that young any more yourself, in spite of those surprisingly dewy-eyed, *ingénue* looks,' he replied, uncrushed. 'Most people subscribe to the wisdom that youth is a poor substitute for experience.'

'Yes, well, I happen to prefer younger men,' Anne said, thinking that if she was going to lie she might as well go the whole hog. She longed to snatch Ivan back out of Hunter's powerful arms and wondered how to do it without risking more physical contact.

'Like Dmitri?' he asked, taking her off guard.

'Who?'

'The baby's father,' he clarified wryly.

'Oh, him. Yes.' Out of an inexplicable desire to shock him she said blithely, 'Dmitri was so young and handsome...' She gave what she hoped was a blissfully reminiscent sigh. 'Barely out of his teens...' She cast him a sly look from under her lashes. 'No experience but *tons* of youthful energy and enthusiasm!'

There was an answering smoulder in the dark eyes during the short silence that followed. Uh-oh, had she laid it on a bit thick?

'No experience at *all*?' he drawled at last. 'Did you take advantage of an innocent young lad, then, Anne? Seduce him before he realised what was happening?'

The idea was highly comical—the blind leading the blind. Her mouth curved, displaying a dimple in her left cheek, and her eyes danced, very blue under their winging brows.

'Oh, I don't have to seduce men. They usually find me irresistible.' She laughed at the absurdity of the notion and tossed her head, the glossy rope of hair snaking forward over her shoulder, revealing the frivolous red bow that bound the end of the plait.

'So you whistle and they eagerly dance to your tune?'

'Oh, no, *I'm* the dancer. I simply teach *them* to whistle the right tunes,' she said pertly.

His gaze followed the red bow as it bounced to rest against her hip. 'A thoroughly devious, manipulating woman, in fact.'

The way he said it, in that slow, gravelly rough tone, it sounded dangerous and daring. Anne rather liked the idea of being considered dangerous, she who had always been boringly safe. Apart from the joyful absurdity of it, maybe if Hunter thought she was a vamp who enjoyed ensnaring helpless victims in her scheming toils he would be more inclined to give her a wide berth and stop pestering her with questions she didn't want to answer.

'Exactly. So you'd better beware,' she drawled throatily, recalling the old movies that her mother had loved to watch on video while she was still imprisoned in her bed. She fluttered her eyelashes at him. 'I might decide that *you* could do with a music lesson.'

He didn't turn a hair. 'I suspect our divergent musical tastes might prove an insurmountable stumbling-block, but thank you for the offer,' he murmured politely. 'If I'm ever desperate for light relief I'll know where to come.'

Light relief? Was *everything* he said a *double-entendre* or was it her sinful subconscious at work again? 'It wasn't an offer,' she snapped.

'No? A threat, then.' He made it sound negligible.

'More of a friendly warning,' she said, hanging on to her patience by a thread. Whatever had happened to that volatile temper of his? Why was he suddenly so frustratingly difficult to provoke?

'Kind of you. But as you pointed out I'm no longer in my first flush of impulsive youth. I doubt if you'd find me as susceptible as a teenage virgin.'

The casual dismissal of her womanly wiles sounded very much like a challenge and for a moment Anne was tempted recklessly to accept it. Fortunately, however, her innate common sense came to her rescue. Taunting Hunter had been asking for trouble; pitting herself against him further would be the equivalent of kneeling down and begging for it!

'May I have Ivan back now?' she asked steadily.

'Why? He's happy where he is.'

He was. He lay cradled in Hunter's big arms as if he belonged there, staring up, wide-eyed, at the dark, jutting profile. One plump fist was stuffed in his mouth and he was sucking noisily, providing Anne with the perfect excuse.

'He's hungry. It's time for his feed.'

'What does he eat?' He swept a comprehensive look across at her empty kitchen. She suddenly remembered she had told him she had her dinner on.

Later, Anne attributed her stupidity to pure panic. She was afraid that Hunter was going to insist on staying until she had answered all his questions. She just wanted to get rid of him—fast.

'He mostly still drinks. Milk. I . . . I'm feeding him myself.'

She was horrified as soon as the words popped out of her mouth. She stared at him, aghast, and could feel herself going beetroot-red as he stared back. A faint answering colour bloomed beneath his olive complexion as his eyes were drawn inexorably back down to her chest.

'I see,' he murmured, and she was too shattered to ask him just what it was that he saw. 'Isn't he a bit old for that?'

'He's only seven months. A lot of women breast-feed their babies until they're a year or more,' she said, numbly trotting out the knowledge she had acquired from her much thumbed child-care book and trying desperately to ignore the focus of that speculative male curiosity.

He frowned. 'But he already has teeth. He could hurt you.'

Oh, God, he actually looked worried at the prospect. He would be demanding an inspection next! 'Babies don't bite, they suck,' she choked. 'It's an instinctive survival mechanism. Now, why don't you——?'

'He bit my finger quite hard,' he pointed out with an infuriating single-mindedness.

'Yes, well, a finger poking around in his mouth is obviously quite different from—from...' She floundered to a halt, overwhelmed by the indelicacy of the conversation. She took a deep breath to try and calm herself. 'Look, if you find the subject so fascinating I suggest you get a book out of the library. I have better things to do than stand here and try to explain it all to you.'

'So you do.' He blinked slowly, and thankfully his attention shifted. He smiled ruefully down at his chubby burden. 'Well, since I can't offer to be of any assistance...'

Anne thought that if she got any hotter she was going to explode. She had a devastating vision of those big, dark hands peeling back her clothes and guiding a baby's head to her naked breast. Their baby. 'Certainly not!'

Her gasping protest jerked his head up and his smile widened mockingly at the sight of her brilliantly shocked eyes. 'Pity.'

He held Ivan expectantly out towards her and she couldn't refuse to take him without looking foolishly skittish. Her instinctive wariness proved justified, however, as Hunter's hands brushed her breasts, lingering deliberately this time, she was sure.

She was even more certain when he said, with patent insincerity, 'Sorry.'

She would have liked to smack his mocking face, except that that would have been the action of an outraged virgin rather than a sultry vamp.

'Don't let me keep you,' she said sweetly, adding with a touch of malice, 'I do hope your dinner isn't burnt to a crisp by now.'

'It won't be. I flicked the elements off before I left,' he said, revealing an aggravating forethought. 'I might have to cook another batch of fettucine, though. How long does it take you to feed Ivan?'

Was this a test? Anne had no idea. She had skipped that section of the book since it was irrelevant. She wondered whether the natural method was any swifter than the artificial and then decided it didn't matter. Hunter wouldn't know the difference either.

'About twenty minutes, depending on whether he's fussing or not...'

To her relief he left without further discussion and she was able to give Ivan his bottle and some mashed banana and warm custard while telling him how impossibly interfering and bossy their neighbour was. She could tell that Ivan agreed by the way his mouth gaped at the catalogue of Hunter's faults.

She was kneeling on the floor, drying him off after his bath, when she heard a staccato rap on the door.

She sat back on her heels, pulling a face at Ivan who lay kicking joyfully on the towel. 'Now, who do you suppose that could be?' she sighed. 'I thought he went off rather too meekly. He's probably brought the spotlight and thumbscrews this time.'

She had underestimated him. He had brought something far more prosaic... and persuasive. Dinner.

He didn't even wait for her to open the door. Before Anne had risen to her feet he had strolled in, bearing a large covered chafing dish and an already opened bottle of red wine tucked under his arm.

'You should lock your door,' he said with irritating complacency as he set his burdens down on the table.

'You were the last one out of it,' she said sourly. 'I didn't know you were coming back or I would have made sure it was barred and bolted.'

'I invited you to dinner, remember?' He came over to stand beside her, his thigh almost brushing her shoulder as he looked down at the cheerfully threshing baby.

'And I distinctly remember refusing,' she replied, but her rejection lacked enthusiasm. She knew she didn't stand a chance against that air of steely determination. Besides, she *was* hungry, so why shouldn't she let him feed her? Perhaps he even meant it as a peace-offering, she thought with unwarranted optimism as she folded the nappy across Ivan's hips, deftly avoiding his churning legs.

Knowing she was being closely observed made her uncharacteristically clumsy. 'Ouch!' She had jabbed herself with one of the safety-pins and dropped it on the floor as a small spot of blood welled out of her thumb.

Hunter crouched down beside her and picked up the pin, nudging her aside with his broad shoulder. 'Here. Let me. You set the table.'

She watched suspiciously as he completed the task with surprising speed. 'Have you got nephews and nieces?'

'I'm an only child. I do, however, have a functioning brain and reasonable hand-eye co-ordination. What goes on next?'

Oh, so he thought it was that simple, did he? She rose to her feet and told him, then lingered to watch, hoping to find something to criticise, but he was as quick and competent at the task as he seemed to be at almost everything else and she found herself fascinated at the way the big hands handled the wriggling baby's uncooperative limbs, gently but firmly threading them into the stretchy towelling sleep-suit.

'Will he go to sleep now, or watch us eat?'

As if he understood, Ivan tucked a thumb in his mouth and looked at them through drooping eyelids.

'Well, he doesn't usually go to sleep right away,' Anne lied.

Ivan closed his eyes and an angelic smile slackened around the thumb.

'That tooth will probably keep him awake for ages,' she added hopefully.

Ivan began to snore.

Still crouching, Hunter swayed back to look up at Anne's frustrated expression, the muscles of his thighs bulging against the taut linen of his trousers with the action. 'Mmm. If you think we need a chaperon perhaps we could prop his eyes open with toothpicks.'

'Don't be ridiculous,' said Anne, although he wasn't far off the mark. It wasn't a chaperon she wanted, it was a distraction. Spending the evening as the sole focus of Hunter Lewis's suspicions was hardly her idea of relaxing.

Once again she discovered that she had underestimated him. For all his volatile temper and impatient directness, Hunter now proved himself capable of alarming subtlety.

While she tucked Ivan into his cot and wheeled it into the bedroom Hunter found the crockery and cutlery, apparently as at home in her kitchen as he was in his own. There were no wine glasses, only tumblers, and when she sat down Anne found that only one of them contained wine. The glass in front of her plate was brimming with chilled milk.

'I know breast-feeding mothers are advised to avoid alcohol,' Hunter commented piously when he saw her brief frown. 'I hope you don't mind my drinking in front of you?'

'Of course not,' said Anne, longing to dump the milk over his know-it-all head. She loved good red wine but was rarely able to afford to drink it and the bottle he had brought was a Premier Cru. She sneaked another wistful look at the label as she picked up her glass and glumly sipped her milk.

She cheered up as she tucked into the fettucine, remembering at the first, heady taste of sauce that he had added a good slug of red wine to it, probably from that very same superior bottle. She relaxed even more when Hunter began to talk casually of trivialities, entertaining her with some pithy descriptions of campus life. Anne was entranced, tipsy with the knowledge that this was now her world too, and she was soon chattering with her usual friendly enthusiasm, so that she hardly noticed when the conversation crept around to the personal. As long as they kept away from the subject of books and writing and Ivan she was cheerfully under the illusion that she was revealing nothing about herself as she talked about her mother's accident and the years of recovery, her father's love of the land and the character quirks of her four rowdy brothers.

'You sound like a very close family.'

'Do we?' Anne had never thought about it before. They were just...family. 'I suppose so...if that means that we're always there for each other. Isn't yours?'

He ignored the invitation to be similarly confiding. 'And were they there for you when Ivan was born?'

Alarm bells began to ring. Anne concentrated intently on her plate, winding a curl of fettucine around her fork. 'They all love Ivan as much as I do. He's my parents' first grandchild, you know. Don is engaged and Rex and Ken have steady girlfriends, but late marriages seem to run in the Tremaine family. Mum and Dad didn't get married until they were...' She stopped, aware that she was starting to babble under that steady, dark-eyed stare.

'How did they feel about your coming to Auckland?'

'Oh, they were glad for me,' she said truthfully. 'Mum especially. She knows I always wanted to go to u——' she had been about to say 'university' and switched it to, 'You know—uh, the city and write...'

'They must miss you both.'

'Oh, I didn't live at home any more, anyway,' she said hurriedly, crossing her fingers under the overhanging rim of her plate. 'But yes, they must do—I've received a letter from home practically every other day!' She laughed to counteract a small pang of homesickness. 'I don't think it really sank in for them that there might be anything to worry about until I had actually left.' All her parents' worries had at that stage been directed towards Katlin. They trusted Anne to behave sensibly whereas they despaired of ever understanding the behaviour of her unpredictable sister. 'Mum's never lived in a city in her life but suddenly she's an expert on life in the fast lane. She keeps sending me newspaper and magazine clippings about coping with life in the urban jungle and I get regular care packages of home cooking. She has this vision of city people as cold and uncaring. She doesn't seem to realise that the people here are the same as they are anywhere else, there are just more of them...'

'An innocent abroad,' Hunter murmured. 'No wonder they're worried.'

'Hardly an innocent,' Anne said tartly.

He looked at her under dark brows. 'Hardly an urban sophisticate either. A sophisticate protects herself. You don't even remember to lock your door, let alone use the most intimate form of self-protection.'

It took a heartbeat before she realised what he was talking about and in a flare of temper she forgot she was supposed to be avoiding the subject. 'What makes you think I forgot? Maybe I wanted to get pregnant!' she snapped.

'Why? To trap your Russian virgin into marriage?'

'No, for the experience of motherhood,' she parroted Katlin's astonishing explanation. 'How can I write from a true female perspective if I haven't experienced the completeness of being a woman?'

He froze in the act of raising his glass. 'You got pregnant as an intellectual experiment?'

Her first reaction was purely instinctive and she quickly tried to disguise her exclamation of shocked distaste. '*No*! I mean, yes—I mean, of course it wasn't quite that deliberate, but . . .'

He drank, watching her over the rim. 'Somehow I can't see you being that calculating. Maybe that's what you tell yourself now, but I think the truth is that you lost your head in the heat of passion.'

Anne's eyes flashed pure gold. 'I never lose my head.'

'Really?' he drawled disbelievingly.

'Yes, really.' A clever idea occurred to her as he continued to regard her with obvious scepticism. 'I save all my passion for my writing,' she said loftily.

'How disappointing for Dmitri.' He looked amused rather than impressed. 'In that case I look forward immensely to reading your book,' he continued smoothly. 'When do you expect to finish it?'

'I don't. I mean, I haven't given myself a deadline, I just go with the flow. And I don't like to talk about work I have in progress,' she said, forestalling any further question. 'It drains the—er——'

'Passion? The creative juices?'

Was he laughing at her? She looked at him with narrowed eyes but his were rounded and innocent.

'Does Ivan usually sleep all night?' he said casually as he poured himself another glass of wine. His third, she mentally counted, and wondered whether the faint glitter in his dark eyes was the beginnings of drunkenness. Certainly he seemed a great deal less aggressive.

'Why?' she asked warily.

'Because I want to know whether my plan to ravish you right here and now on the floor can proceed without interruption.'

She winced at the irony in his voice. 'He's always slept through the night.' She couldn't help looking at the hard, polished floor out of the corner of her eye and frowning. It would have to be very uncomfortable, particularly with a man as big as Hunter...

'I'd let you get on top,' he said silkily, catching her out in her mental gymnastics and causing her clear, sun-gold complexion to bloom.

To her relief he didn't pursue her embarrassment. 'Is that the real reason you prefer writing at night? Because it's the only time you can get uninterrupted peace? Why don't you just pay a baby-sitter during the day?'

'Because I can't afford to.' She was still distracted by her furtive imagination, trying to damp down the awful little thrill prompted by an image of herself dominantly astride that big, muscular body.

'I understood that the grant is pretty generous. Certainly enough for you to afford day-care.'

'I can. Ivan stays at the university crèche——'

'Only when you're in class. I would have thought it was more important for you to free up your writing time——'

She woke up suddenly to the trend of the conversation. 'I told you, I'm best at night.' She jumped to her feet and began to clear away the dirty plates. 'Speaking of which, I suppose I'd better get down to it.'

He rose meekly, but getting rid of him wasn't so easy, she discovered, as he insisted on helping her with the dishes while he finished his wine.

'Just don't think this means I'm coming next door to help you wash your pots,' she warned him, her attempts at polite denial giving way to a flat-out rudeness to which the man seemed equally impervious.

'I wouldn't dream of thwarting the nightly flow of your passion.'

Her toes curled in her shoes at the teasing remark. 'At least I don't have to worry about you driving home,' she grumbled as she filled the sink with hot water.

'Would you worry?' he asked, moving up behind her.

'Not about you, but about others you might meet on the way,' she said bluntly. 'My mother's accident happened when a drunk ran into her. He got off with a few scratches, the loss of his licence and a couple of months of periodic detention while Mum got seven years of confinement and pain.'

'I'm sorry.' His quiet sincerity took her off guard and she turned, just as he moved to pick up the tea-towel on the bench beyond her. Trapped against the cupboards, Anne could feel every inch of him from chest to knee...every impressive inch! 'Anne?' He picked up her plait, which had flopped on to the bench, winding it around his hand as she maintained her silent resistance, forcing her to look at him. 'I'm sorry.'

She meant to say something flippant, something smart, something sophisticated. Instead she could only stand there, transfixed by the dark compassion in the heavy-lidded gaze, aware of simmering heat that had nothing whatsoever to do with the sultry, late-summer night.

And then he kissed her.

CHAPTER FIVE

SHE might have known that something would go awry. After all, nothing so far in her life had gone precisely to plan—why should kissing be any different?

Anne pushed the button on her tape-deck and grinned at the staccato sound that issued. She turned up the volume and directed the speaker towards the wall so that the incessant typewriter tap-tapping mingled with a similar sound issuing faintly from the other side. She cocked her head as the distant echo faltered while hers continued with machine-gun precision.

Aha, she thought smugly, dusting off her hands as she left the bedroom, let Hunter *now* accuse her of not working hard enough!

She went back to her Russian text, sprawling on her stomach on the floor beside Ivan's cot, surrounded by her books, but found it next to impossible to concentrate. She sighed and pillowed her chin on folded arms, her drying hair sprayed like a damp blanket across her back, providing a cool relief from the sultry evening air that wafted in the open window.

She hadn't had any trouble concentrating on that damned kiss. It had absorbed her whole being. A week later, just thinking about it still made her go warm all over. Nothing in her unadventurous past had prepared her for the impact of all that concentrated masculinity on her senses. Funny, she had never thought of herself as being a particularly sensual person. Hunter Lewis had changed all that.

She closed her eyes as she remembered with a stab of satisfaction that Hunter had seemed every bit as shaken by their kiss as she had been.

She had seen the faint look of surprise in his dark eyes when his head had bent towards hers, as if what he was doing had caught him completely unawares. Then her thoughts had been scattered under an avalanche of sweet sensation...

His fist tightened on her plait, pulling her head back, and she instinctively went up on tiptoe to meet his descending mouth. It was hard, hot, and faintly hostile. Instead of frightening her, his restrained aggression was fiercely exciting. He wasn't asking for a response, he was demanding it, and Anne gave with greedy generosity. When he bit at her soft lips they parted instantly and he plunged inside, making a rough sound of triumph that vibrated on her tongue. He tasted deliciously warm and spicy, and as he sank recklessly deeper she pressed her palms flat against his chest to steady herself and was entranced by the straining tension in his body, the rapid, erratic pounding of his heart. Her hands slid to his sides, fingers curling jerkily into the taut muscle as he made another primitive sound and shifted, crowding her closer against the cupboards. His thighs tangled with hers, his hips pushing, forcing her to acknowledge his superior strength and aggressive maleness.

He tugged her hair, using it to control the angle of her mouth against his, adjusting her so that he could penetrate her more thoroughly, arching her throat so that his free hand could run down the vulnerable length of her, from jaw to flank and then slowly back up again to stroke the velvety skin of her throat with a threatening deliberation. His fingers trailed lightly against the sensitive flesh, teasing her with an unbearably gentle possessiveness until his thumb found the betraying throb of her pulse under the point of her jaw and pressed into it so deeply that she felt dizzy, more dominated by him with every heartbeat. She uttered a tiny, melting moan of confusion and his mouth let her go, but only long enough for her to blink at him in dazed disappointment, her eyes slumberous, her tender mouth a languorous invitation. His bruising expression flared into one of white-hot satisfaction and then he was back, burrowing into her moist heat, using his tongue to explore the completeness of her submission to his masculine aggression, his hunger so intense that he was shaking as much as she.

His hips anchored the centre of her body while his stroking fingers drifted leisurely down from her throat and over the honey-smooth slope to the soft elastic of her blouse, tugging at it until it dipped below her lace-clad breast. His palm was warm and dry, creating a delicate friction as he cupped the fragile lace and shaped her to his touch. Oh, yes, this was what she had needed. She arched herself into the pleasurable new sensation and his fingers tightened, his thumb moving to rub insistently back and forth across the firm crest of her breast until Anne felt she was going to burst with exquisite agony.

'Oh, please...' She shuddered as his mouth moved to nip at her ear and exposed throat. His fingers paused in their magical work and she cried out in soft protest. 'Oh, no... please... don't...'

To her horror he released her breast entirely. 'Are you still tender from feeding Ivan?' he murmured raggedly. 'Are your breasts too swollen and sensitive to be touched...?'

'Oh, no, I meant don't stop,' she begged incoherently, dragging his hand back to her breast, taking over the role of the aggressor as she pulled his head down and began kissing him eagerly, using her tongue the way he had shown her.

She pushed her hands eagerly up under his shirt to stroke his silky, hot, hair-roughened chest. She touched his flat, masculine nipples and was startled to feel them react sharply, hardening under her clumsy caress. Intoxicated by a rush of feverish curiosity, she pulled her mouth away from his and pushed the soft fabric up out of her way, revealing the thick muscles bunching and shifting with every convulsive breath.

'Anne...'

She was too enraptured by her discovery to notice the husky note of warning in his voice as his hand stilled on her breast.

'Why, you're just like me,' she murmured wonderingly, touching a finger lightly to one rigid nipple where it peeped out of its thick nest of hair and watching it stiffen further.

He shuddered and swore savagely under his breath and she looked up at his face, fascinated by the mixture of smouldering resentment and carnal desire that she saw there.

He was fighting against *her*, she realised with a quiver of shock—against what she could do to him. But she wasn't his enemy and she wasn't about to let him shrug off what had just happened between them as a momentary aberration!

Holding his smoking black gaze with dreamy intentness, Anne leaned forward and pressed her open mouth over the stiff brown button of his nipple. His reaction was gratifyingly swift. As she began to suckle he gave a hoarse cry of shock, his head jerking back and his jaw clenching, his whole body tautening and lifting towards her.

He made the mistake of looking down at her again, seeing her watching him with those provocatively knowing eyes as she feasted on his flesh. Her tongue flicked over him in a wicked, velvety rasp and he went rock-hard at the involuntary image of her sinking to her knees and using that sultry, skilled mouth on him in other, even more pleasurable ways...

'No, damn you, that's enough!' He dragged himself out of her reach, staggering slightly as he turned away to readjust his clothing, leaving Anne bereft and feeling somehow betrayed, an angry frustration clawing at her insides.

He swung back and stiffened at the sight of her dishevelled figure, a sweet disorder of femininity. Her wistful expression of wanton dismay seemed to spark an even greater rejection.

'Cover yourself!' he rapped out curtly.

When Anne's fingers fumbled with the elastic neckline of her blouse he uttered a brief imprecation and pulled it sharply up, taking care not to touch her silky skin, snapping the elastic firmly back into place at an overly modest height before moving quickly out of her reach again.

Anne almost smiled in sympathy. If Hunter was feeling anything like she was right now then she could understand the rawness of his temper. But, after all, it was entirely his fault that they were both feeling frustrated: *she* wasn't the one who had cried halt.

She eyed him warily, noting the rigid posture, the fists clenched at his sides, the black scowl. His whole attitude was a picture of stubborn rejection as he avoided her gaze, dark colour streaking his rugged cheekbones. Was he embarrassed at his lack of control? Or was it self-disgust that robbed him of his usual blunt, head-on approach to awkward situations? Or—ghastly thought— was it *Anne* he was disgusted with?

'There's no need to get so uptight, Hunter,' she said, endeavouring to project a non-threatening breeziness that she didn't feel. 'We didn't do anything wrong. We were just having a little fun——'

'Fun!' It was the wrong word to use. Hunter looked as if he was going to explode.

Pride made Anne refuse to back down. 'Yes, fun. You know, Professor, when you do something purely for pleasure, amusement, diversion . . .'

His explosion was brief and to the point.

'Well, I suggest that in future you look for your amusing little diversions somewhere else, because I'm not in the market for your cheap brand of fun!'

'Cheap?' Anne was bewildered by his fierceness. 'We were just kissing, for heaven's sake. You think I go around kissing every man I meet?' she asked, torn between offence and laughter.

The urge to laugh was stifled at birth as he rapped out forcefully, 'If you think what we were doing was "just kissing", then that explains Ivan. No doubt you and his father were "just hugging" during his immaculate conception——'

Anne flushed deeply at the unfairness of it. 'Don't you dare bring Ivan into this!'

'I dare because it's evident that you haven't learnt very much from your past experiences . . .'

'There wasn't much to learn . . .' she said bitterly.

'Oh, no, I forgot—you gave lessons to them.' He flung her foolishly teasing words back in her face.

'That was a joke. You can't believe I meant it?' she cried incredulously.

'Can't I? What other lies have you told me that I shouldn't believe?' She flinched and he smiled sardonically. 'This time the joke's on you, sweetheart; you can't plead virtue with a mouth as skilled as yours. You were practically eating me alive.'

Anne was stricken. He made her eagerness sound so sordid, as if he had been merely a passive victim of her lust, instead of the prime instigator.

'Oh, I see, I should have pretended not to notice when you grabbed me,' she said furiously, placing the blame squarely back where it belonged. 'Sorry I got it wrong. You should have told me that lack of enthusiasm is what you require from your women, and I would have dropped off to sleep instead of trying to liven you up!'

'The last thing I need is livening up,' he ground out. 'And don't flatter yourself that you'll ever be *my woman*... There's more to being a woman, thank God, than the ability to have sex and babies—something you've evidently yet to discover!' He punctuated the scathing exit-line by violently slamming the door after him.

Looking back, it was obvious to Anne that her flippancy had been the trigger for that whole, bitter exchange. She should have been calm, serious, not tried to hide her insecurity behind joking words, but that had always been the way that she coped with life's unexpected blows—by turning them inside out and rendering them harmless with her fine sense of the ridiculous. Besides, it was pretty difficult to act calmly when you were shaking like a leaf.

She propped herself up on her elbow again, brushing damp strands of hair off the page in front of her as she frowned down at the Russian phrases that mocked her comprehension.

On second thoughts, taking their brief encounter seriously would probably have achieved exactly the same result, only faster. University gossip had it that the dynamic professor had only rarely been sighted with the same woman twice, which only added fuel to the wild rumours: that he was secretly having an affair with another professor's wife; that he was a misogynist; that he was a satyr who could never be satisfied by one woman; that he was a closet gay; that he was suffering from a bad case of unrequited love or still carrying a torch for his dead wife.

Of all the rumours, Anne was willing to give credence only to the last. Some judicious shaking of the grapevine had revealed that Hunter had been a widower for over five years, his wife having died while they were living in Australia, and yet his extreme reticence about his marriage seemed indicative of some deep, unresolved feelings. As he was hot-tempered, demanding, impatient and articulate, it had to be a very powerful emotion that was capable of inhibiting his natural expressiveness. If he still felt loyalty to the memory of his wife, that would explain his violent denial of any attraction towards Anne. He had certainly been avoiding any chance of a recurrence, by being singularly elusive.

Unfortunately, it seemed that every time Anne *had* seen Hunter since that night, she had been welcoming or farewelling a different male, and of course he hadn't given her the chance to explain the entirely innocent circumstances. No, he had merely given her one of those hooded stares, oozing with suspicion, which seemed to have become his speciality...

On Rachel's advice, Anne had put up a card on the university library bulletin-board advertising the massage skills that she had acquired while nursing her mother and, somewhat to her surprise, had found herself with a small but regular trickle of clients in the shape of brawny student sportsmen who couldn't afford professional physiotherapy treatment for their minor injuries but who, if they couldn't come up with the very modest fee she charged, were willing to swap services which to Anne were even more valuable than money.

Thus she had quickly acquired two terrific male babysitters—a catering student who cooked her gourmet meals and a rugby player who chauffeured her to the shops and back. Then there was the trainee sound-technician who had made her the typing sound-effects tape, no questions asked!

Twisting sideways to flip impatiently through her Russian-English dictionary, Anne caught sight of her exercise mat rolled up in the corner of the room and was instantly revisited by last night's infuriating débâcle.

All Hunter's worst suspicions about the parade of impressive physical specimens to her door must have been confirmed the previous evening, when he had brought her some mail which had been left in his letterbox by mistake.

Anne had just finished strenuously working on her rugby player, whose thigh had been over-stressed by some typically macho posturing on the weight machines at the gym. It had been hot, and she had stripped to a singlet-top and shorts, her skin damp with perspiration. Jerry, who had been wearing even less, had rolled over on the floor and started pulling on his faded tracksuit bottoms as she'd answered the door.

Handing her letters over, Hunter's eyes had flicked briefly past her to the man scrambling into his clothing and the rumpled sheet spread out over an exercise pad on the hard floor.

'Been having *fun*, Anne?' he murmured silkily.

'Actually no, it's very hard work,' she replied evenly, determined that this time she would not let the situation degenerate into farce. She would explain clearly and succinctly what was going on and Hunter would stop looking at her as if she had just crawled out from under a stone.

'Not for me.' Jerry had got to his feet and now sauntered up behind her, his cropped gym shirt still in his hand, acknowledging the man at the door with a nonchalant disrespect that revealed his engineering school origins. Cocooned by the sciences, he had never had to worry about facing Professor Lewis's legendary temper on a personal basis. 'All I have to do is lie back and let myself be mauled by this little tiger,' he grinned, and suddenly his overgrown-puppy personality was less endearing than usual.

'No one can make me feel as good as Annie can. She's got a magic touch,' he burbled on, slinging a broad, naked arm around her neck and hugging her back against him. Jerry had already made the obligatory pass—on his first appointment—and had taken his rejection with cheerful unconcern, so Anne knew that his action was merely friendly. But with Hunter's hawkish gaze on them she felt awkward and tried to squirm discreetly out of the casual embrace. Unfortunately Jerry didn't know the meaning of discretion and thought himself excruciatingly witty.

'Hey, quit wriggling around like that, Annie,' he said in an oily, mock-leering voice. 'You might give the professor the wrong idea about us...'

As if he didn't have it already! She was tempted to slap his face for what she read in the narrowed black eyes. Did Hunter really think she had so little self-respect? And so much stamina! She studied all day, looked after Ivan, supposedly wrote all night—where she was supposed to get the energy for all this frantic sex he seemed so keen to think that she constantly indulged in?

'Jerry's studying engineering... He plays rugby for the university,' she began tightly. 'I was just——'

'Running through some plays with him?' Hunter interjected smoothly.

To her annoyance Jerry pre-empted her cutting response with a laugh and a friendly slap on the flank. 'She just can't keep her hands off me, can you, Annie? But I must admit she's getting me in great shape for the touch season.'

'How apt,' Hunter said with cool sarcasm as he looked at the beefy hand where it had come to rest against the pale, rounded thigh revealed by Anne's frayed denim shorts.

'Well, don't let me interrupt any further,' he drawled, turning on his heel with a thin smile. 'By all means go back to your... tactile exertions...'

'He was talking about summer touch rugby,' yelled Anne at Hunter's retreating back, but he ignored her, the back of his head and set of his wide shoulders as expressive of contempt as his coldly insolent smile had been. If it weren't for Jerry looking interestedly on she would have marched after him and insisted that he give her a proper hearing. Dammit, one day she was going to demand that he stand his ground and back up these ridiculous notions he had about her!

What really fretted her was that he might have knocked on her door for a reason other than just to deliver her letters. After all, it would have been more in keeping with his current policy of isolationism to have left them in her letterbox, or on her front doormat. Instead he had chosen to make personal contact.

But if the gesture had been a small olive-branch then he had certainly snatched it back with unflattering alacrity! It was almost as if he had *welcomed* a further excuse to despise her.

Anne sighed heavily again, her pen tracing absently over the Cyrillic script in front of her. She persevered valiantly for a few more minutes, but finally she threw the ball-point down in disgust and sat up.

'This is ridiculous!'

Since she obviously wasn't going to be able to get any serious work done until she had confronted Hunter, she had no choice. She'd just have to bite the bullet and *beg* for the opportunity to watch him grovel.

She was almost out of the door when she remembered her typing tape still chattering away and rushed back to switch it off. The sudden cessation of noise woke Ivan and as she picked him up it occurred to Anne that Hunter might need some softening up. To talk properly with him she would first have to get invited in, and perhaps Ivan could do that for her. She could say that she needed to look up an all-night chemist in his phone book so that she could get some more gel for his gums or something...

Ivan looked suspiciously calm and drowsy for a supposedly fractious baby but Anne decided to chance it. The worst that Hunter could do was to shut the door in her face.

If he opened it in the first place, of course!

Standing outside in the narrow hallway, knocking on his door for the fourth time, Anne found herself getting annoyed. For a grown man Hunter was acting very immaturely, hiding in his room like a sulky child. He should come out and take his punishment like a man!

'This is the last straw!' Anne told Ivan grimly as she marched back down to the cupboard where the fuse boxes were and felt in among the rusty nuts and bolts in a small cardboard box. The key was there, where Hunter had advised her to leave a spare of hers when she had locked herself out of her flat one day.

'I suppose this is an unforgivable invasion of privacy,' she murmured to Ivan as she quietly inserted the key into Hunter's front door, and was delighted to feel it smoothly unsnick the lock. 'If not actually illegal...'

Ivan's head loyally bobbed back and forth as he gabbled his views on the individual's right to privacy. Anne shushed him and he shushed moistly back, making satisfying bubbles. She couldn't resist popping one with her finger, which made him blink in astonishment then go squinty-eyed with glee.

'Hunter?' She pushed open the door and then was impatient with her own tentativeness. 'Hunter!'

She held Ivan protectively in front of her, half expecting Hunter to rush out of the darkness at full throttle.

Darkness?

There were no lights on in the flat, although jazz played quietly somewhere...complex, soulful, extravagant. Rather like Hunter himself, thought Anne nervously.

Perhaps he had already gone to bed. But surely he couldn't be asleep, not with her so-called typing racketing away in his ear? And she had been knocking loud enough. No, he was just ignoring her and expecting her to creep away like the moral criminal she was.

Anne fumbled along the wall for the light-switch, wincing as she knocked a frame askew in the process. The row of pendent lights flicked on along the length of the room. The antique desk under the vaulted windows was empty; an electronic typewriter with a sheet half rolled through the platen stood abandoned on the cluttered surface. Anne was drawn irresistibly towards it, holding her breath as she tiptoed closer and leant over to read the typescript.

Her eyes narrowed. It was a passage about the current state of Soviet politics, but it wasn't in the crisp, factual style of a lecture or a text. She shifted a few of the completed pages next to the typewriter.

She almost dropped Ivan.

It was a novel. Some kind of political thriller, judging from the paragraphs she had read, and a well-written one at that, the prose taut and streamlined, yet oddly lyrical in its rhythms.

Oh, *hell*, he *was* a writer! No wonder he had asked so many questions about her book. She hunted for the title page with the author's name.

Lewis Hunt.

She had no sense of instant recognition. Well, perhaps he wasn't published yet, she thought hopefully. Her eyes strayed to the bookcase immediately beside the desk and her hopes sank without a trace. Lewis Hunt's name was printed on the spines of three glossy-jacketed hardback novels, and there were several political texts by Hunter Lewis, including a history of Soviet politics. No one had told Anne he was an author, but perhaps it was such common knowledge around the university that everyone assumed she knew.

Next to his own books was a row of books on Russian history and culture—in Russian, of course. Anne's self-confidence was dwindling by the minute!

She flipped morosely through the loose manuscript again and her eyes widened as she came across an unexpected love-scene. Her mouth formed a little O of shock as she became riveted by the graphic description of the hero's fierce coupling with a woman he knew to be his enemy. It went on for two pages and was a highly erotic piece of writing, especially when she mentally substituted Hunter for the hero. Anne was breathing hard as she hurriedly tucked the pages back in place. Goodness, what an imagination he had, or was the description drawn from his own experiences?

The thought made her suddenly loath to enter his bedroom. What if he was furious? What if he reacted as his hero had in that scorching scene and tumbled her face-down on to the bed, binding her hands with one of his silk ties so that he could...?

Ivan disrupted her delicious speculation by blowing another bubble in her ear and starting to chew on a strand of her hair. No, she was safe with her tiny witness, Anne decided regretfully. Besides, mothers of teething babies were hardly likely to be mistaken for beautiful, blonde, karate-kicking Valkyries whose passions were as excessively developed as their pelvic muscles!

The darkened bedroom was also empty, although Anne noticed with a *frisson* when she turned on the light that the bed itself was the same kind of slatted wood as the one described in the manuscript, even down to the convenient posts at the head to which a man could tie a woman...if he was so inclined.

Swallowing nervously, she automatically switched off the radio on the bedside table in the interests of saving electricity, and in the instant of quiet which followed she heard a rattle at the front door and remembered that she hadn't closed it behind her.

She shot out of the bedroom and stopped dead at the sight of the woman who was setting a soft carry-all bag beside one of the squashy apricot leather chairs.

She was tall and lithe, an ash-blonde, and as she straightened up again Anne could see that she was also beautiful in a very sophisticated, strong-featured way. A veritable Valkyrie, in fact, dressed with dramatic flamboyance in an emerald silk suit.

And not to be trusted, decided Anne arbitrarily. A pushy, expensive, hard-faced tart who was out for everything she could get. And definitely too old for Hunter. Forty at least, she estimated jealously.

'Hello, have you come to see Hunter? I'm afraid only Ivan and I are home. Can I help?' she said sweetly, before it suddenly occurred to her that Hunter might have gone out to fetch this hard-faced tart in his car and would soon appear himself.

Astonishment was vivid on the other woman's face as she looked at Anne's long wet hair and bare feet, her loose, drop-waisted white Indian cotton dress and the dark-featured baby at her hip.

Then she smiled brilliantly and Anne's hard-faced tart theory gurgled down the drain.

'Hello. It doesn't matter; Hunter wasn't expecting me. I just dropped in on the off-chance. You know, this door wasn't even closed, let alone locked. Not exactly wise, even in a neighbourhood like this.'

She came closer in a graceful glide, the brilliance of her smile softening as she pulled a little face for Ivan and earned herself a chuckle.

'You sound just like Hunter,' said Anne involuntarily.

'Oh, dear, how depressing!' Brown eyes twinkled as they transferred back to Anne. 'Is he still unbearably bossy?'

Anne's jealousy writhed briefly again and died. 'Well, more *bearably*, actually, considering how much he gruffles and growls when he doesn't get his way.'

'"Gruffle"—what a lovely word, and just perfect to describe Hunter when he ruffles his brow and makes those menacing grumbles in his chest. I'm glad to see you aren't intimidated by his temper. So *bad* for him, I feel, to think he can use it to manipulate us. We haven't met before, have we? My name's Louise.' She held out her hand, long-fingered and strong, her palm surprisingly rough against Anne's.

'I'm Anne——'

'With an "e", of course?' The grin was vaguely familiar, the dark-pencilled eyebrows arching as they invited the affirmative answer.

'How did you guess?'

'Apart from the fact that I read all of *Anne of Green Gables* when I was a child?' The teasing look suddenly changed to one of dauntingly shrewd analysis. 'You're more complex than first glance suggests. You have the innocent mask of youth, of course, but there's a hint of mystery around the mouth and eyes—as if you're constantly guarding secrets. A Mona Lisa air... serene but secretive. And all that lush hair... Hunter has always had a fetish about women's hair. No wonder he was attracted...'

Anne was unnerved both by her perspicacity and her generosity. It made her own jealousy seem petty and mean. 'Uh, Louise——'

'Have you lived with him long?'

'No—that is, we're not——'

'Oh, don't worry.' The smooth blonde hair bounced against her firm jaw as the other woman shook her head reassuringly. 'I know you're not *married* ... Goodness, he wouldn't have kept *that* a secret. I must admit I'm a bit miffed about this darling boy, but no doubt there's a perfectly reasonable explanation.' She studied the baby with evident satisfaction. 'Ivan. I like that. May I hold him?' She was already reaching out with obvious eagerness.

'Uh—of course.' Anne handed him over, still trying to make sense of Louise's previous comments. 'Would you like to sit down? He's quite heavy.'

'No, we're fine. How old is he?'

When Anne told her she nodded. 'Big for his age, but then so was Hunter as a baby.' The emerald-silk arms held the baby with an easy familiarity that belied the careless sophistication.

'Hunter?' For a confused and dreadful moment Anne thought that this woman and Hunter had had a child together—his namesake.

'Of course Hunter insisted on being born early,' Louise continued without waiting for a reply to her tart remark. 'So typical of his impatience. He wanted to get on with real life, not hang around wasting valuable time in the womb. No thought of the considerable inconvenience to *me*, insisting on being born on the Waiheke car ferry! His father was sure they were going to try and charge us for an extra ticket when we disembarked. But that was Paul all over... always busy anticipating trouble before it occurred. A marvellous organiser but a disastrous husband for someone who abhors being *organised...*'

Anne blanched. Louise. L.L. The signature on the paintings!

'Are you...? But surely—you can't be Hunter's *mother*!' she wailed, repudiating the thought of such a terrible gaffe.

'Oh, dear,' Louise said drolly. 'Can't I? Someone had better tell Hunter he's been sending Mother's Day cards to the wrong person all these years.'

'But you're far too young!' Anne protested.

Louise laughed, revealing wrinkles where there had been none before. 'Thank you for that delightfully sincere piece of flattery, Anne. Now you know why I only make flying visits to Hunter. He ages me dreadfully. I was practically a child bride, you see, but I'm nearly fifty-five now. And you, young man, are going to age me even further,' she fondly scolded Ivan, who seemed as fascinated by this colourful apparition in his life as Anne was dismayed.

'You know, you look just as Hunter did at your age, except that Hunter was a brooding baby. He hardly ever cried,' she added to Anne with a warmly reminiscent smile, 'but he had this glare that practically shrieked. Of course, the lack of smiles made each one that much more precious. People used to run themselves ragged trying to coax a smile from him, so he never ran short of entertainment. So you see, your daddy was manipulating people with his temperament even then...' Louise sat down and bounced Ivan gently from side to side on her knee as she teased him.

'Oh, no—you don't understand!' Anne was horrified by the realisation that Louise thought that Ivan was her grandson! 'Hunter and I aren't really living together. I live in the flat next door——'

Louise cut her off happily. 'An excellent arrangement ... I know just how you feel—I need lots of personal space too. Unfortunately Hunter's father couldn't give it to me in the context of our relationship. He was such a *conventional* man. Thank goodness Hunter seems to be more flexible——'

'No, really—Mrs Lewis—Louise.' Anne's voice rose frantically as she cut to the crux of the misunderstanding. 'Hunter is *not* Ivan's father.'

Louise seemed amused by her vehemence. 'Are you sure? There's a fairly unmistakable likeness.'

Her hopeful expression made Anne almost feel guilty for disappointing her. 'It's just coincidence.' And as Louise opened her mouth again Anne said flatly, 'Hunter and I have never even slept together.'

'Not even once?' his mother asked wistfully. 'You didn't both get a bit carried away one day and go further than you meant to...?' She paused as Anne went tellingly pink and vocally applauded with glee. 'Oh, you did! I'm so glad! So maybe there is a tiny element of doubt...'

Before Anne could firmly quash any such suggestion a dangerous drawl came from the door. 'A tiny element of doubt about what, Mother?'

Hunter was home, and he was not in a good mood.

CHAPTER SIX

'I REALLY am awfully sorry,' said Anne earnestly, over the top of a large, artfully designed menu.

'So you said.' Hunter's neutral calm seemed to project a high degree of scepticism as he studied the dessert restaurant's printed offerings.

'No, really, I am. I had no idea she was your mother.' Traces of her earlier surprise still lingered in her voice.

'Oh? So who did you think she was when you drifted out of my bedroom in your see-through nightie and boldly flaunted our love-child in her face?'

'It wasn't a nightie, it was a sundress, and I never said that Ivan was yours,' Anne denied hotly. 'Your mother jumped to that conclusion with no help from me.'

His black eyes suddenly lifted to capture hers. 'I notice you don't dispute the see-through bit,' he said.

Remembering the way his gaze had crawled over the thin white Indian cotton dress, Anne took a hurried sip from the glass of iced water in front of her and tried to appear insouciant. 'Just be thankful I was wearing underwear!'

It was difficult to maintain the brazen front when he murmured unexpectedly, '"Thankful" isn't the word that instantly springs to mind.'

'Anyway, when your mother appeared I thought...' Anne hesitated. 'Well, she's very attractive, isn't she? And she doesn't look like you—I mean, she's blonde for a start...' She could hear herself floundering, and so could Hunter.

He slowly put his menu down, a strange light dawning in his dark eyes. 'She's been dyeing her hair for as long as I can remember—blonde is simply her current colour. And yes, she is an attractive woman.' He studied Anne's uncomfortable expression for a few seconds longer. 'Did you think my mother was my lover, Anne?' he purred.

She flushed guiltily. 'I told you, I didn't know who she was...'

'But you decided to make trouble for me anyway,' he said silkily.

Anne lifted her chin. 'All I said was that you weren't home.'

'Thereby subtly establishing your role as female-in-residence. No wonder my mother started piling on the conclusions—she knows I prefer living alone.' A slow smile widened his square mouth. 'I wish I could have seen your face when you realised the audience you were playing to. Mum has always been the type to prefer audience participation to passive observation.'

'So I discovered,' said Anne ruefully. 'I truly tried to straighten her out when I realised, Hunter, but she just seemed to take over the conversation...'

'Another one of her great talents. Witness our being here.' He looked around the small, elegant waterfront restaurant which specialised solely in extravagant desserts.

As if he had signalled, the waiter appeared at his side and took their orders, Anne waiting impatiently for him to depart before she replied aggressively, 'You didn't *have* to agree to come.'

'Neither did you,' he pointed out mildly. 'We could have both stayed home and continued the conversation with Mother.'

Anne shuddered and Hunter gave her a small, ironic smile. He knew as well as she did that she had been so desperate to extricate them from the awkward situation in the flat that she had literally dumped Ivan and run when Louise had gaily suggested that she act as baby-sitter so that the two of them could go out for the rest of the evening.

All Anne had seen was a chance to get Hunter away from his mother so that she could explain the embarrassing misunderstanding. Not that Hunter had seemed embarrassed. After his initial, brief burst of restrained fury when he had realised that Louise had discovered Anne in his flat, he had blatantly enjoyed his revenge, an infuriatingly silent witness to Anne's harassed efforts to persuade Louise that she had the wrong end of the stick about Ivan.

'Darling, you never told me about Ivan!' Louise had chided him when he had sauntered menacingly into the room. She had been cheerfully undaunted by the furious black eyes that had sliced between the two women and made Anne quiver.

'Element of doubt about what?' he repeated tautly, bending over the baby in her arms to kiss his mother's proffered cheek.

'I was just telling Lou—your mother—that we don't have that kind of relationship,' Anne interjected hastily.

'What kind of relationship?' asked Hunter, straightening, the grimness in his eyes altering slightly as he took in her flushed agitation and his mother's wickedly angelic expression.

'You know,' mumbled Anne evasively, not wanting to put it into words.

'I don't think I do,' he said uncooperatively, his eyes narrowing as he took in her floating hair and dress. It covered her to mid-calf but somehow, with Hunter looking at her like that, she felt naked.

'I was just remarking on how alike you and this little sweetheart are.' His mother interrupted the long, smouldering stare.

'And I was just telling her it was pure coincidence——' Anne began repressively.

'Hardly pure, Anne,' Hunter commented, destroying her frail attempt at regaining some of her normal composure.

'Will you shut up?' she snapped and then bit her lip. 'I'm sorry; as I said to your mother, you and I hardly know each other...'

'She's afraid I'll be shocked and disapproving just because she let slip that you both got carried away by your passions one day,' added Louise helpfully. 'You'll have to convince her, Hunter, that I'm not some sort of maternal ogre. Really, Anne, I do admire people who refuse to be slaves to convention...'

'Is that what you told her, Anne, that we lost our heads and were careless?' he murmured with a sulphurous smile.

'Of course not!' she denied urgently, and Louise came unexpectedly to her defence.

'She merely blushed in the right places, Hunter, and I drew my own conclusions.'

'And here was I thinking you were an utterly brazen, unblushing hussy,' said Hunter softly, not taking his eyes off Anne, and his mother gave a little crow of laughter which was echoed by Ivan.

'You know, I'd like to paint this little man some time,' she said, her thoughts darting down another byway. 'With you too, Anne. I've never done a Madonna—maybe I could try it with a modern twist...' she mused.

Anne hated to think what that modern twist might be and evidently Hunter's thoughts were running along similar lines because he took another oblique jab at her composure.

'A nude Madonna, Mama? What a good idea,' he purred. 'Anne is a very modern, free-thinking woman and she certainly has the body for it.'

Mother and son looked at Anne for a long, silent moment and she ached to turn the tables. 'Have you ever done a nude of Hunter, Louise?' she asked recklessly. 'He has superb muscle-tone for a man of his age.'

While Hunter's eyes snapped, his mother's twinkled. 'Only ink sketches of him as a baby. He had a lot more dimples than muscles then, of course! I shall show them to you some time, Anne, and we can compare notes. I haven't seen Hunter nude since he was about thirteen...have I, darling? That's when he got his first attack of adolescent modesty and he never quite seemed to shake it off. I hope he's not still repressed on that score, but of course if you've been admiring his body, Anne, I suppose he must have loosened up considerably...'

'Mother——'

'I gave up on Deborah, I'm afraid...she was far too *spiritual* a person to plumb the earthy side of Hunter's nature—so *serious* all the time. People with no sense of humour should never get married. A little reckless irresponsibility now and then does us all good, don't you think, Anne? Hunter especially needs the safety-valve of laughter because he has the awful combination of a passionate temperament and an over-developed sense of responsibility that insists he must always be in control——'

'*Mother*! Did you come here expressly to psycho-analyse my life, or is there another reason for this surprise visit?' he asked sardonically.

'I'm off to Los Angeles tomorrow to oversee the setting up of my exhibition,' his mother relented. 'I thought you might put me up on your luxurious couch for the night. You know how I hate hotels and I need a good snooze before the flight.' Her eyes flitted back to where Anne stood, grateful at being out of the spotlight.

Perhaps her relief was too obvious, because Louise Lewis suddenly back-tracked again. 'Speaking of which, I don't think we actually settled the little matter of Ivan's paternity.'

This time Anne was better prepared for the verbal ambush. Her observations of mother and son had made it evident that tact and diplomacy were not required. 'Hunter and I only met a few weeks ago,' she said bluntly. 'So you see he couldn't *possibly* be the father.'

'You mean it's an *inconceivable* notion.' Louise laughed at her pun, stroking Ivan's silky black curls and adding with a wistful shrug, 'Oh, well, maybe next time...'

Next time? Before Anne could make the mistake of repeating it as a query, Hunter intervened.

'Why this sudden eagerness to thrust fatherhood on me?' he asked. 'You always said one child was enough for you.'

'For me, yes. I have my art. Not for *you*. You're not a naturally solitary person, Hunter, you're a people person—that's why your books sell so well. And you have a very enviable capacity to concentrate on a multiple of levels. You like to be in the thick of things. I think you need a woman who will drive you crazy trying to keep up with her, and lots of children to love and drive you crazy too. You'd make a wonderful father... don't you think, Anne?'

Anne fielded her bland look warily, fascinated by these illuminating parental insights, remembering the gentle patience with which Hunter had handled Ivan, but also recognising another potential minefield. 'Uh, well——'

'You can stop mentally measuring her hips, Mum,' drawled Hunter. 'She comes from good country stock and is proven fertile. I'm sure I can breed from her at the drop of a hat.'

'Hunter, there's no need to be crude,' his mother reproved while Anne spluttered furiously.

'You should be so lucky!' she got out eventually and Hunter had the gall to laugh.

Louise noticed her restraint. 'If you two want to really let rip, I can look after Ivan while you go next door and do it in privacy.'

'The walls are too thin,' said Anne automatically. 'I—I mean, you'd be able to hear every word we said unless we whispered,' she stammered as Louise looked mightily amused, making it obvious that it wasn't words she thought she might hear.

'Is it Ivan you're more concerned about, or me? I could wear ear-muffs, but Hunter will tell you I'm pretty much unshockable.'

'Shocking but unshockable,' he confirmed with a wry smile of affection. 'And I don't own any ear-muffs.'

'I could turn the radio up!' she offered mischievously. 'But no, that would disturb Ivan, wouldn't it . . . ? Look, I think he wants to go to sleep. I know! Why don't you two go out on the town while Ivan and I have an early night? Sublimate all that sizzling hostility with food. My agent told me about a *fabulous* new dessert restaurant on the waterfront; you could go there—chocolate is supposed to be a great sublimator. My treat, of course . . . And by the time you get home, well, Ivan and I'll probably be fast asleep so you can have as much privacy as you want. Otherwise . . . well, I suppose we can all stay here and have a nice, cosy chat. You can tell me *all* about yourself, Anne, darling, where you came from and who your family is . . . and all about Ivan, of course . . .'

That clinched it. Anne practically fled back to her rooms to drag on her trusty 'basic black' dress, bundle up her hair and sketch in her face and trundle the cot back to Hunter's so that Louise could put Ivan down in his familiar bedding. If he had been old enough to talk she wouldn't have dared leave them together for she had no doubt that Louise would have wheedled the truth out of him in no time flat!

Louise, with her mile-wide unconventional streak, would probably find the story vastly amusing, but her son...just the thought of his reaction made Anne's heart thump violently in her chest. She absently adjusted the little sleeveless red silk jacket that cleverly dressed up the plain, strapless black sheath, unconsciously re-assuring herself that her nervous reaction wasn't visible.

'Are you all right?'

She almost jumped. 'I beg your pardon?'

'Are you feeling uncomfortable? Do you have to feed Ivan again soon?'

She grinned reminiscently. 'Oh, no, he gorged himself to bursting-point at dinner. I couldn't stop the little devil. I have the feeling he's heading for a life-long fixation.' She was remembering his delighted discovery of a novel new taste: baked beans—painstakingly inspected one by one and blissfully consumed in the same way.

'I don't blame him. I'm a breast man myself.'

Anne's mouth dropped open at his forthright reply and she went pink as she recalled what Ivan's chief source of sustenance was supposed to be and realised what Hunter had meant by his polite query, and the interpret-ation he must have put on her reply. She became aware of her hands fiddling with the edges of her jacket and snatched them away, which had the unfortunate effect of thrusting her breasts into stark prominence. Hunter's hooded gaze took advantage of the exposure to study the generous, curving slopes revealed by the straight-cut bodice.

'My mother's right, you do blush in all the right places,' he murmured mockingly, and she knew without looking down that her chest was as rosy as her face. She hunched her shoulders, which merely had the effect of deepening the interesting cleavage.

'And you're looking for a punch on the nose!'

'If you're going to wear dresses cut to your navel you have to take the consequences.'

'Don't exaggerate. I've had this dress for years and no one has ever called it low-cut before.' She wished she could accuse him of dressing to accentuate his sexuality too, except that there was nothing overtly sexy about the conservative dark jacket, white shirt and tie. It was simply the man beneath the clothes.

'There's your explanation. Doubtless it wasn't designed for feeding mothers. You look as if you're going to pop out of it at any moment.'

So maybe she *had* put on a pound or two since she had bought the dress. She didn't have the money to go around splurging on new clothes each season.

'I never have yet,' she muttered.

'There's always a first time,' he said virtuously. 'All it would need would be a little accidental tug and the waiter would have no need to ask if we wanted whipped cream with our chocolate.'

'Accidental tug'? The glitter in his eye was anything but virtuous and for a fleeting moment she was strongly reminded of his mischievous parent.

'Don't you dare! And I am not a cow!' she gritted.

'That wasn't what I meant,' he murmured gently. 'I was referring to the creamy colour and texture of your skin. It really is incredibly pale for a country girl. I thought you were all supposed to be nut-brown country maids.'

'Well, you were wrong on both counts, then, weren't you?' she said tartly, disconcerted by his teasing admiration. 'Haven't you ever heard of the hole in the ozone layer? Nut-brown country maids are likely to get skin cancer these days. Besides, I spent most of my time inside...'

'Ah, yes, with your writing...'

Anne mentally rolled her eyes. Out of the frying-pan into the fire. A teasing, sexy Hunter was difficult enough to handle; a serious, interested professional was even worse!

'I suppose that's why you don't have much of a tan, either,' she attacked. 'Writing those riveting thrillers of yours must absorb all your spare time.'

He leaned back in his chair to allow the waiter to set their desserts on the table. Hers was huge, a compendium of chocolate delights. His was modest in comparison—freshly diced fruit to be dipped in a dish of chocolate fondue. He watched her plunge in with sensuous abandon before picking up his fork.

'Do I detect a hint of sour grapes there? You've never mentioned my novels before. Usually budding authors are all over me with eager questions.'

Anne let a spoonful of chocolate mousse dissolve in her mouth before she allowed herself to respond. 'How tiresome for you. No wonder you were annoyed when a literary neophyte moved in next door. I'm glad I politely restrained myself from fawning at your famous feet.'

His mouth kicked briefly upwards at her acidic alliteration. 'I doubt you would ever fawn—or that self-restraint came into it. You've only just made the connection between Hunter Lewis and Lewis Hunt, haven't you?'

'Since I've never read any Lewis Hunts there was no connection to make,' she said crushingly.

'I must lend you one to read,' he said mildly. 'So how *did* you find out...?' He trailed off, his eyes narrowing as Anne hurriedly buried her intrusive nose in a chocolate cup.

'I noticed the books in your bookcase... and saw the manuscript on your desk,' she added in a low mumble.

'You mean after you broke in you did some snooping,' he translated crisply.

'I didn't break in—I used a key!' she pointed out. 'And it wasn't to snoop. I thought you were still home and just refusing to answer the door. I'd heard your typewriter, you see——'

'Over the deafening sound of yours? I *am* surprised,' he said drily. 'That's why I went out. I found I couldn't concentrate under the sudden deluge of your creative juices so I went up to the roof to think out some problems in peace.'

So that was where he had been!

'Old machines are noisy,' she countered hurriedly. 'Anyway, I was wondering whether to wait until you came back——'

'In my bedroom?' he asked smoothly. 'Isn't that where Mum found you?'

'I thought you were in there,' she said weakly.

'Really?' His eyebrow shot up and his mouth curved tauntingly. 'I'm flattered.'

'You know what I mean!'

'Again, no, I don't. You have the distinction of being the most incomprehensible female I've ever met. I just think I have you pinned down and you spring another surprise on me.'

'What a relief,' she said, not altogether jokingly. 'At least I'm not boring. Look, if I were out to seduce you I wouldn't try to do it with a babe in arms, would I?'

'A lot of men find motherhood erotic.'

'Do you?' she couldn't resist asking.

He tilted his head, studying her silently, his reluctance evident. Suddenly she had her answer and it was a deeply intriguing one. She leaned forward, resting her chin on her hands, intrigued by the notion. 'You *do*, don't you?'

'In the abstract, I suppose it's an instinctive male response to the concept of feminine ripeness——'

He had adopted a detached, lecturing tone and she wasn't going to let him get away with it. 'We're not talking abstracts.'

'Aren't we?' He concentrated on swirling a speared piece of kiwi fruit with thick chocolate sauce.

'No,' she dared. 'We're talking about *me*.'

Chocolate sauce dripped on to his hand and he licked it off, lifting his lashes again just in time to catch her mid-shiver.

His discomfort melted visibly away. He leaned across the table, offering her the chocolate-covered fruit on the end of his fork. 'By all means let's talk about you,' he agreed with a velvety smoothness that was so unnerving that she opened her mouth and let him tease the sweet morsel inside. 'What is it you really want from me, Anne? Why did you come over tonight?'

She chewed with unknowing sensuality as she struggled to cope with the hidden invitation in his eyes. 'I wanted to explain about Jerry—and the others...'

She sensed his immediate withdrawal even before his face visibly chilled. 'How you live your life is your own business.'

'Yes, that's sort of what it is,' she grasped eagerly at the opening. 'A business.'

'Another "experience" you need for your writing?' His voice was icy with distaste.

'No, it's because I know I can't rely on the grant money to see me all the way through university,' she admitted frankly, 'so——'

'So you're willing to prostitute yourself for your education? Oh, I'm sorry, you're called "sex workers" these days, I believe,' he apologised with thinly veiled contempt.

Anne gaped at him. 'What *are* you talking about?'

'You and your Johns. Or do you call them all Jerry?'

The penny dropped. He didn't think her merely promiscuous, but mercenary as well! If she hadn't been so outraged she would have laughed. 'I wasn't selling them sex, you moron, I was giving them *massages*!'

The middle-aged man at the next table turned his head in sharp interest and Anne ducked her head and hurriedly lowered her voice.

'A physiotherapist at the hospital where Mum had her operations taught me therapeutic massage so she wouldn't have to resort to pain-killers as much!' she told Hunter fiercely. 'Jerry and the others are athletes, for goodness' sake, and if you say, Yes, sexual athletes, in that supercilious tone of yours I'll empty this bowl of chocolate soup over your head.'

'You would too, wouldn't you?' he murmured, eyeing her fists clenched on the sides of the small dish. He spread his hands, palms uppermost, with a rueful shrug. '*Mea culpa* What was I supposed to think?'

He believed her. Just like that! Perversely, Anne was annoyed by his belated trust. 'You were *supposed* to give me the benefit of the doubt.'

'As you did me and my incestuous mother?' he turned the tables neatly to enquire.

Anne blushed. 'That was different.'

'Yes. There's only one Louise. You, on the other hand, had a whole string of virile young men panting to your door. And what about that tubby, ageing bikie who was pounding on your door on Monday night? You can't tell me he's a sportsman.'

'He's a friend of my eldest brother. Don seems to have lined up some of his Auckland mates to check up on me every now and then. I'm sorry if he disturbed you.' Her level stare made it clear that she thought he had deserved it.

'They *all* disturbed me,' he obliged her by admitting. 'You didn't have your music turned up quite loud enough to cover the grunts and yelps and groans. It sounded as if your strapping young men were in the throes of delirious ecstasy.'

Anne laughed. 'More like agony. It's amazing how wimpy the average macho male is about minor aches and pains. If we were making so much noise I wonder you didn't yell at us to pipe down. You never hesitated to do it before.'

'I didn't want to put you off your stroke,' he said, reddening very faintly.

'Why, Hunter,' she teased, 'did you have your ear pressed to the wall?'

The colour on his face deepened and to her delight she realised that the sophisticated Hunter Lewis had indeed acted like a curious adolescent.

'You must have wondered why *I* was always so quiet,' she pursued him unmercifully, and couldn't resist the dig, 'Did you wonder whether I let them tie me up and gag me?'

'Are you going to eat that or play with it?' he said gruffly, referring to the wafer-thin slices of white chocolate she was breaking up with her spoon.

She picked up a thin sliver in her fingers and brushed it back and forth across her moist lower lip. Hunter followed the movement with dark-eyed envy, mixed with a wariness that she found emboldening. 'Do you want to share?' she asked huskily, unable to believe her own foolishness. But flirting with Hunter, Anne was discovering, was quite as addictive as eating chocolate. One taste simply wasn't enough.

'It's unhygienic,' he murmured distractedly.

'Not if you shower first.'

He blinked. 'Anne...'

There was a trace of helplessness in his protest that was irresistibly alluring. She touched his hand where it lay on the table, running her fingers over the pad of his thumb to curl into his palm and stroke back and forth.

'Would you like to exchange private fantasies with me, Hunter? You never know, we might find that we share the same one...'

So lost was she in a fantasy of her own—that she had him so off balance she could tease him with impunity—that she was stunned when Hunter's strong fingers suddenly wrapped around hers.

'What a good idea, Anne. Why don't we do just that? After all, my mother has given us *carte blanche* for the entire night; we can spend it on a fascinating voyage of mutual discovery...'

CHAPTER SEVEN

THE theory of sublimation was just so much hot air, Anne thought raggedly as she sipped her liqueur coffee and nibbled desperately on a chocolate-covered mint wafer. She had eaten everything in sight, including dipping into Hunter's left-over fondue, and she was still sizzlingly aware of the man across the table.

And he wasn't doing anything to help. All the while they were talking of other things—innocent, innocuous, everyday things—he kept letting those hot, dark eyes wander all over her upper body, staking a claim, making her feel thoroughly self-conscious and flagrantly female.

Her teasing flirtation had got her into trouble and she had not the first idea of how to extricate herself . . . or even if she wanted to. Ever since he had made that outrageous proposition, her delicious uncertainty had grown. Had he been joking? Or was he as serious as his body language suggested?

'Does your mother visit you often?' she asked, seeking the most mundane of subjects to try and cool her increasingly heated speculation.

'Only often enough to disrupt what she calls the "comfortable complacency" of my life,' Hunter said wryly, stirring his coffee. He took it plain, she noticed, black and bitter. 'She travels a great deal. Although she has a home in Wellington she has artist friends all over the world who provide her with studio space whenever she wants it.'

'That's what I want to do.' Anne's eyes were full of dreams. 'Experience different cultures at first hand by living in them instead of having to read about them in books. Languages are going to be my passport. When I get my degree I'm going to apply to the Department of Foreign Affairs, maybe even become a UN translator...'

'I thought you wanted to be an author?'

Anne bumped back to the ground. 'Art doesn't recognise national boundaries. If your mother can do it, so can I.'

'I do see a certain resemblance,' Hunter murmured, and watched her eyes flicker in dismay. She reminded him of his *mother*?

'I'm nothing like your mother!'

'Maybe not in looks——' Anne's anxiety subsided a little '—but you certainly have her eternal, exhausting optimism.'

'Because I've learnt that believing the worst will happen is a powerful reason for giving up on life,' said Anne fiercely, thinking of her mother who had, in the early days after her accident, come close to accepting the medical opinion that she would probably never walk again. 'You're an optimist too, even if you don't want to admit it, or you wouldn't write books where the hero triumphs in the end. You'd write gloomy, turgid tomes that pander to the intellectual snobbery that insists that only the certainty of death and the misery of human suffering make literature worthwhile——'

'Pax, pax.' He was laughing, catching her waving hand in both of his. 'Calm down. I wasn't criticising you—it was merely an idle comment...'

'None of your comments is idle,' she retorted, trying to ignore the way he was gently separating her fingers. 'They work very hard at being cryptic.'

'What was so cryptic about saying you're an optimist?' he asked, turning her hand over so that his fingers slid between hers.

'It was the *way* you said it,' she insisted darkly.

He lightly restrained her hand when she would have tugged it free. 'Why do you find it so difficult to accept that I might admire and envy your joyful confidence that life will treat you kindly?'

She looked at him through her lashes. To be admired and envied wasn't what she wanted from him, but perhaps it was a start...

'You didn't think I was so admirable a couple of hours ago...'

'I didn't know you as well then as I do now,' he said mockingly. 'And a couple of hours from now perhaps I'll know you even better...'

Anne blinked. 'You can be very silver-tongued when you want to be,' she muttered warily.

If only she had the experience to judge whether his words were an invitation or merely idle teasing. She didn't want to mistake sophisticated flirtation for red-hot desire and embarrass them both by bursting prematurely into flames. She was fairly close to spontaneous combustion as it was!

'It was an essential qualification in my first career. I was a military attaché at several diplomatic postings.'

He couldn't have chosen a better way to divert her from her self-doubts.

'You were in the *army*?'

Anne was stunned, although, come to think of it, his physical and mental toughness could well be a hangover from military training. It would also explain that irritating habit of expecting people to jump to his orders.

'I went through university on a military scholarship,' he confirmed, his smile acknowledging the silent question immediately evident in her eyes as he continued. 'That was in the days when we suffered in genteel poverty for the sake of Mum's undiscovered genius. When she started achieving success she offered to buy out my commission but I figured that I owed the army their minimum five years after I graduated, especially when they offered me post-graduate studies at Duntroon after my officer training.' The prestigious Australian military academy explained the puzzling abbreviation that had accompanied his degree in the calendar that Anne had consulted. 'I minored in military history and tactics and made sure there was sufficient language content virtually to assure me overseas duty——'

A light went on in her head at his overt blandness. 'Let me guess. Russia!'

He inclined his head in amusement at her envious exasperation. 'My speciality was Soviet—now post-Soviet—politics.'

'You speak Russian, don't you?' she accused. 'I bet you're as fluent a speaker as you are a reader. All those books in your bookcase... You *knew* I was taking Russian but you never said a word——'

'Because I don't give private tuition,' he cut her off in his clipped, professional tone. 'To *anyone*. I have enough on my plate. But you're welcome to borrow any book that you think might be helpful to you.'

Instead of taking offence at his stand-offishness, Anne found herself in complete agreement. Hunter was enough of a distraction when he was nowhere in sight, let alone shoulder to shoulder, mind to mind. The only private lessons that she would like from him had nothing to do with academics! Still, she owed it to her god-child to know something of the land of his father.

'How long were you in Russia?' Her fingers tightened on his in unconscious demand. 'Have you been inside the Kremlin? Seen the armoury...?'

By the time they were driven out of the restaurant door by the staff's pointedly sweeping around their feet Anne was starry-eyed with determination that she would one day see the country that Hunter had brought alive for her so vividly. No wonder he was a successful writer; he had a gift for communicating not just the concrete reality of a place, but the emotional impact of it too.

It wasn't until they were walking back up the hill towards the warehouse that Anne realised that the underlying tension between them was back in full force. It had never really gone away, merely been masked by a more acceptable form of enthusiasm.

'Perhaps we should have brought your car,' she said, breaking the unnerving silence. Although he didn't seem to use it often, she knew he had a cream-coloured Mercedes which he parked in the rental garage two buildings away from the warehouse.

'The walk will do us good after all that cholesterol,' Hunter replied, cupping her elbow to guide her across the deserted street. Under the bleaching, blue-white street-lights he looked almost like a stranger, hard-faced and remote. 'Are you afraid?'

Just in time she realised that he meant of the city at night. 'No, it's just that it smells like rain.'

'Are you hoping for a polite discussion of the weather all the way home to avoid more personal topics?' he asked, with his usual skill at sensing her nervousness.

As he spoke a very fine mist of moisture began to drift gently down around their shoulders, haloing the overhead lights with reflective streamers. He laughed softly as he urged her into a run towards the first of the row of huge plane trees that marched towards the university, their pale, piebald trunks rising from the black tarmac where the street had been widened around them— nature victoriously fighting back against the encroachment of the city.

'What is this—witchcraft? Or are you taking meteorology as a sideline?' he said, slowing to a brisk walk, his grip sliding naturally from her elbow to her hand.

'Which would you prefer?' Even under the thick canopy of rustling leaves the haze of moisture swirled in their faces, but it was a warm and sensuous rain that was at once caressing and cleansing.

'I think I'd prefer a scientific explanation but I suspect you'll have a more romantic view.'

'There's nothing wrong with being romantic.' Anne took issue with the cynical edge to his words.

'Not unless it's confused with something else. Then it can have painful consequences.'

She was panting a little to keep up with him. 'Are you warning me not to get romantic about you, Hunter?'

He shortened his stride abruptly, half turning towards her. 'Do you need to be warned?'

She tossed her head, inadvertently loosening the casual French twist that anchored her slippery-clean hair. 'That could be construed as a very arrogant thing to say.'

He stopped in the shadow of a towering trunk, their linked hands jerking her to a sharp halt that caused her hairpins to dislodge further. 'Is that a yes or no?' he demanded tautly.

'Which would you prefer?' she asked again, mocking him with the altered context.

He was relentless, his other hand grasping her shoulder and giving her the hint of a shake. 'Just answer me, dammit! Why are you being so evasive?'

Suddenly she was angry with him for trying to force her into analysing her feelings as if they were a research project she was submitting for an exam. They were feelings, for goodness' sake, they didn't *have* to be logical. They were *supposed* to be wild and wonderful.

'To avoid having to confess that I've fallen madly in love with you, of course,' she said with a sweet malice that she knew he would instantly discount.

Sure enough he made an impatient growl. 'You really like playing with fire, don't you?'

'Haven't you noticed I'm a little singed around the edges?' she said throatily, raising her free hand and

loosening his tie before he could stop her. It made him
look as reckless as she suddenly felt. After the way he
had looked at her in the restaurant it was a little bit late
to issue warnings! 'I hate the cold, don't you, Hunter?
I'd far rather burn than freeze...'

She flicked his collar button open and brushed her
fingers against the hard collarbone, the taut sinews of
his throat. Her thumb sank into a vulnerable hollow.
His pulse was thundering as wildly as hers. Anne went
weak with relief. She wasn't sure how far she could carry
this brazen overture without some responsive
encouragement.

With a movement that was blurringly fast he caught
her hand and whipped it aside, moving forward at the
same time so that their bodies collided with a cushioned
force that sent Anne stumbling backwards into the
nearest tree. When she caught her breath again she found
herself trapped against the smooth bark, caged by
Hunter's hands firmly planted on either side of her
narrow shoulders and the looming bulk of his body.

'Hunter!' In spite of her exultation that she had
sparked a response, *any* response, she wondered apprehensively whether she had pushed him too far.

'Anne...' His face was in shadow, his eyes faint,
glimmering slits in the dark that were no more expressive than his voice.

He said nothing more and the silence stretched, along
with her nerves. Only the occasional car passed up the
hill and there were no other pedestrians. Over the hushed
fall of rain she could hear his breathing keeping pace
with hers, fast and uneven. What was he waiting for?

Anne's nerve broke first.

'Hunter, we're in a public place. What do you think
you're doing?' Her demand was weak as she saw the
whiteness of his teeth flash. She shifted, her one good
pair of heels grating against the tree roots, one shoe

turning so that she had to clutch at his shirt to stop herself pitching sideways, dragging him closer in the process. He didn't protest, his torso crushing hers, his head lowering with deliberate slowness until his reply feathered against her lips.

'What *you* want me to do...'

Dammit, she wasn't going to let him make this seduction sound totally one-sided. She jerked her head aside. 'I never said I wanted to be manhandled——'

He had the audacity to laugh, his breath caressing on her averted cheek.

'No? I never said I wanted to be *woman*-handled, but you went ahead and did it anyway. So stop playing coy. You want this as much as I do.'

At least he was admitting it. Anne slanted him a look from the corner of her eyes. A flurry of leaves parted overhead, allowing a shaft of street-lighting to strike his face, revealing its hungry tension.

'Are you going to make me beg for it, Anne?' he taunted as the shadows cloaked him again. 'Is that the way you like it? Does it take a spicing of humiliation to turn you on?'

Her chin whipped proudly up. '*I* don't have any fetishes!'

'Good, neither do I,' he said, so smoothly that she knew she had just been manipulated, and when she opened her mouth to remonstrate so did he...right over the top of hers.

His mouth was rough and urgent and suddenly the entire length of his body was grinding her sweetly against the tree, his legs crowding against hers, his shoes tangling with her high heels, and impatiently nudging them further apart as he narrowed his stance so that the anchor for her spinning universe was the sharp thrust of his hips.

Anne felt the snag of her pretty jacket against the small splits in the bark at her back but couldn't bring herself to care. What was a ruined dress compared to such bliss? She slid her palms across his silky shirt-front and around his back under his satin-lined jacket. Every inch of him felt taut and aroused and she revelled in the smothering heat that enveloped her as she surrendered to his extravagant demands. He kept her hard up against the tree, as if he was afraid she would escape if he eased the pressure of his body, but Anne was in no danger of running anywhere but headlong into pleasure.

His mouth moved from her hot mouth to her jaw, her throat and the soft curve of her breasts above the strapless dress. Like the subtle rain his touch was moist and mystical, at once soothing and arousing. His thick hair brushed the underside of her chin as he bent to her body, and the hands that had earlier caged her ran restlessly up and down her sides, settling at last on her hips and dragging them forward into the centre of his need. Instinctively Anne lifted her knee, not even feeling the shoe slip off her foot and bounce into the gutter as she pressed the inside of her thigh against his lean flank, like a rider trying to sense the next move of a powerful, unruly stallion.

He made a thick, greedy sound and immediately slid his hand into the crook of her raised knee, tugging it higher on his hip so that he could settle more securely between her legs, trailing his hand up the back of her thigh to cup the curve of her buttock, its smooth roundness tautened by her wanton pose.

His aggression instantly slowed and altered as he made the intimate, unhurried journey over and over again, caressing her thigh and massaging Anne subtly against his rocking hips until she echoed the incoherent sound that he had made, feeling the velvety friction against her bare skin build up into an explosive frustration. She wrapped her leg around him, trying to capture the elusive sensation with the supple flexibility of her body.

Another car passed and even though they were protected by the tree's night shadow Anne felt exposed by the brief wash of light against her closed eyelids. She didn't want to stop but she longed to touch Hunter the way that he was touching her, under his clothes...

She clenched her hand in his hair and choked, 'Hunter, please——'

His answer was to return to her mouth, smothering her murmured protest. 'Please what? Aren't you burning yet, Anne? I am,' he growled huskily.

'We're in the *street*——'

He stroked that same, knowing path with his large hand. 'I've never made love standing up...' he said into the moist cavern of her mouth.

Anne was momentarily diverted. 'Haven't you?' she asked shakily, conscious of the fact that he saw her as a sexy woman of the world and that it wouldn't do to sound shocked. She settled for a vague rendition of the truth... which he would soon discover for himself if things went much further! 'Well, there's a first time for everything.' Her voice sank another sultry octave as she made the honest vow, 'And I can promise you'll experience a lot of firsts with me...'

'I look forward to it.' He licked at the leaping pulse in her throat, a tiny lash of fire. 'I've always been conservative in matters of sex...until now.' His finger traced the delicate line of her panties as he watched her face, avidly enjoying her flagrant response. 'You arouse some very radical desires, but I'm sure you know that. I suppose you're used to driving men to extremes...'

She shivered as the pad of his finger threatened the integrity of the lace-trimmed elastic. If he could make her feel like this she would agree to anything. His hair was thick and silky between her fingers and she inadvertently tightened them again.

'Oh, yes, I do it all the time,' she said hoarsely, arching back against the tree, almost forgetting her misgivings about their lack of privacy until she caught sight of a white car looming out of the misty rain, slowing abruptly as the headlights picked out her lone shoe lying in the gutter.

'Uh, Hunter——' She struggled to wrest her leg from his grasp.

'Mmm...?'

'Hunter, let me go!' She didn't dare struggle when he ignored her ragged plea. 'Hunter, for goodness' sake—it's the *police!*'

She almost fell as he jerked upright at her furious hiss. The blue-striped passenger door of the police car opened and Anne hurriedly tried to smooth down her crumpled dress and re-pin her collapsing hair as a uniformed officer stepped out.

'Are you all right, miss?'

'Uh, yes, fine. Just fine!' said Anne brightly, limping away from the tree, conscious of the other officer behind the wheel observing their encounter with his partner.

'Is this your shoe?' He bent to pick it up, not taking his wary eyes off Hunter.

She took the proffered shoe and wobbled on one foot as she slipped it back on. 'Yes, thank you, it fell off when I—when we—that is, when we...' She became conscious of Hunter standing stiffly at her side and nudged him sharply to indicate that she needed some cooperation.

'When we got a bit carried away,' he responded rather too obligingly.

The young policeman looked from Anne's dishevelled figure to Hunter's tense expression and relaxed slightly. 'Been out for the evening together, sir? Know the lady well, do you?'

Even a naïve country girl could see the trend of his questions, and Anne was instantly outraged.

'He didn't pick me up on the street if that's what you're implying!' she snapped. 'We live just up the road—we've been down to the waterfront to eat.'

'I see.' The young man's smile was close enough to a smirk to be even more annoying.

'For your information his *mother* happens to be baby-sitting for us,' Anne stressed very loudly. 'We're two perfectly *respectable* citizens taking an evening stroll and minding our own, perfectly *innocent* business——'

Feeling Hunter start to shake beside her, Anne put a hand on his forearm, not wanting him to be arrested for assaulting an officer for the slur on her honour.

'Now, be polite to the policeman, darling; he's just doing the job we respectable citizens pay him for,' Hunter said in a voice that trembled suspiciously, and she twisted to look at him, realising that it hadn't been anger sending ripples of tension through his body.

His black eyes laughed at her furious chagrin. 'You should be grateful he stopped to make sure you weren't in trouble. And you must admit that what we were doing might have been perfect for us—but it wasn't exactly *innocent . . .*'

She blushed fierily. 'Why, you——'

'I assure you, Officer, we have no intention of risking an indecent exposure charge.' Hunter spoke hurriedly over her smouldering tones. 'If you excuse us I think we'll just toddle on home to the baby . . .'

'That might be a good idea, sir. Safer for both you and your lady.'

'Not to mention more comfortable,' Hunter grinned, and they exchanged secret male glances before the policeman turned back to his car.

'I can't believe you had the gall to say that!' muttered Anne, torn between a giggle and a glare as Hunter slid his arm through hers and hustled her up the hill in the wake of the accelerating patrol car.

'Neither can I,' he said wryly. 'Put it down to shock. I'm not used to assisting the police with their enquiries.'

'And you think I am?'

'The police, no. The fire department? Possibly. You're a dangerously inflammable woman.'

Her good humour was restored by the distinct note of admiration in the rueful remark. She began to laugh and hugged herself against his side, partly as a protection from the feathery rainfall and partly for the sheer pleasure of it.

A bubble of happiness caught in her throat. Tonight was a new beginning. She had discovered that Hunter possessed a kindred streak of wicked humour that might enable him to appreciate the lighter side of her reckless deception when, as she conceded must inevitably happen, she told him Katlin's story.

'I don't suppose it would have done your academic reputation any good if he had hauled you in front of a judge for consorting with a prostitute,' she teased.

'I don't think there's any such crime,' said Hunter, his arm around her supple back as they leaned into the hill. 'It's the soliciting part that's illegal; the clients get off with a slap on the wrist. You're the one who would have been up on charges.'

'Don't sound so smug. I would have told them *you* were doing the soliciting,' Anne told him as they turned into the dim alleyway next to the warehouse and Hunter unlocked the side-door which they used when the docking bay was closed.

'I bet you would have, too,' he said with a mock-growl, and chased her squealing up the stairs. She whirled around to jeer triumphantly at him when she reached the top, her hair losing its final battle with the pins, flaring out around her as he caught her by the waist.

She steadied herself with her hands on his shoulders, his stance on the step below allowing her to look him directly in the face. What she saw there made her even more breathless.

'I—I wonder if your mother's asleep?' she stammered, glancing towards his door.

He wound his hand around a long skein of hair, tugging her face back towards him. 'It doesn't matter whether she is or not.'

'Doesn't it?'

'No.'

She swallowed nervously at his clipped reply. He looked so... broodingly serious. She didn't know if she was quite ready for this after all. Not yet. Not with the credibility gap yawning between his perception of what she was and what she actually was...

'Hunter——' She decided it might be best to approach it from an oblique angle. 'I—it's been a long time for me...'

He stilled. 'How long?'

Now, tell him *now*!

'A *very* long time...' she forced out.

He drew the most obvious conclusion, his eyes glinting with satisfaction. 'Before Ivan was born?'

She shook her head, smiling shakily. '*Way* before that——'

'Good,' he cut her off before she could formulate the rest of her confession, holding her wide-eyed gaze with dark intensity as he took the final step up and towered over her, increasing her sense of feminine vulnerability. 'So there's no danger of complications from former lovers... on either side, because it's been quite a while for me too.'

His fingers slipped through the satiny strands of her hair, raking it forward over her slim shoulders, the backs of his hands skimming her breasts. 'You have incredibly beautiful hair...' He bent and buried his face in a handful of it.

'Your mother said you had a fetish about it,' whispered Anne, trying not to lose track of her good intentions.

'Is it my imagination, or are you raising the spectre of my mother with oppressive frequency?' He raised his head and pulled her into him for a long, fierce kiss that drove every doubt about the rightness of what they were doing from her head.

'Getting cold feet, Anne?' he said as he released her crushed mouth.

She shook her head dumbly and he smiled savagely.

'You should. Nice girls aren't supposed to go to bed on the first date.'

Anne paled and he swore, stopping her instinctive recoil towards her door with a blocking movement of his body.

'I'm sorry. That was cruel and uncalled for. It was frustration talking. Much as I'd like to fling you on to your bed and make mad, passionate love to you all night long, knowing I can't gives my temper a nasty edge.'

'Why can't you?' asked Anne croakily, liking him even more for that instant, unqualified apology.

'I'm not prepared.' At her blank look he said impatiently, 'To protect you. Since you're still breast-feeding I presume you're not taking an oral contraceptive?'

'I—well, no, I'm not...' She was slightly stunned by the practical turn of the conversation coming hard on the heels of exigent passion.

'And since you've been celibate for so long I presume you don't have any condoms lying around the flat?'

She blushed and shook her head. He smiled grimly.

'I do, but I know my mother will have commandeered my comfortable bed, in spite of her comments about the couch, and I have no intention of providing her with more maternal ammunition by waking her up groping around in my bedside table.'

He ran his hands forcefully up and down her slender back, shuddering as he pulled her against him, letting her feel the surging strength of his arousal.

'Around you I don't trust myself to dabble in a little light-hearted foreplay. It's tough enough thinking logically just holding you like this, let alone when you're responding to me so generously. I almost had you out there against that tree and damn the consequences.' He rested his forehead against hers and continued in a rough undertone, 'I don't want to settle for rushed half-measures, either. I want to be buried deep inside you when I come, so let's wait until we can thoroughly indulge ourselves, mmm? Perhaps tomorrow, when my interfering mother's gone...'

When Hunter left her—with another devastating kiss after helping her transport a sleeping Ivan from his flat to hers—Anne fell into bed still shivering internally at his casually graphic description of what their love-making would be like.

The thought of Hunter buried deep inside her was both thrilling and alarming, and also infinitely desirable, but she was secretly glad that he had given her the opportunity to put off her confession.

Tonight had been for them alone. It would remain a perfect jewel in her memory, untainted by whatever strife tomorrow's truth might bring. For this was the night that she had acknowledged to herself that she was irrevocably in love with Hunter Lewis. He might choose to call it by other names—passion, desire, mutual chemistry—but Anne knew that what she was feeling was greater than the sum of all three. And Hunter...well, at the very least he had admitted a passionate attraction that could well flourish into something deeper and more lasting if she provided the right fertile conditions.

She didn't see Hunter the next morning but she did get a fleeting visit from his mother, who thrust a small framed painting into her hand, declaring that she had a taxi waiting to take her to the airport.

'I *was* going to give it to Hunter, but I've decided I'd rather give it to you,' she said ruthlessly as Anne tried to protest against a gift of such value. 'It's one of Hunter's favourites because it's this little bay up north where we used to holiday when he was a boy. He simply *lived* on that beach...'

'Then you can't just give it to me——'

'You don't like it?' Skilfully pencilled eyebrows rose haughtily and Anne blurted a disclaimer.

'Of course I do.' It was beautiful, a delicate oil that seemed to capture the perfection of a faded, fond memory. In the distance, on the sandy curve of beach, was a small red dot, and Anne instinctively knew it was Hunter as a child, 'father of the man' she loved. She suddenly felt ridiculously close to that tiny dot. As if she was sharing that gritty, sandy, sunny, innocent childhood moment...

'Good.'

'But won't Hunter be upset at your giving it to me?' She didn't want to give him more excuses than absolutely necessary to be angry at her.

'No more than I'm upset with that depressingly ugly experiment of mine that he insists on flaunting in my face,' said Louise drily.

'But, well, it's personal to your family...to Hunter...'

'And so are you, darling.' The haughty brow lowered to deliver a jaunty wink. 'Consider it my contribution to your campaign to drive Hunter wonderfully crazy. Hang it on your wall where he'll see it every time he walks in, and tell him you'll only sell for an outrageous price——'

'I would never *sell* it to him!' Anne cried as Louise turned for the door at the sound of a distant, impatient toot from the street.

Louise grinned over her shoulder. 'I know. But let him find out for himself that love can buy what money can't. Give Ivan a goodbye kiss for me—and Hunter too, for that matter. He left for some meeting at a god-awful early hour and I wasn't really *compos mentis* when we said our farewells...'

Anne's second visitor of the morning was even more of a shock. She simply stared at her sister until Katlin brushed past her, looking eagerly around the flat.

'Where is he?'

'Who?' For an awful moment Anne thought her family knew all about her plans to abandon herself to the ravages of a passionate affair and had sent Katlin to talk some sense into her. Then reality reasserted itself. No one in their right mind would send Katlin to advise common sense over impulse.

Katlin looked at her strangely, her smooth bell of blonde hair quivering as she shook her head. 'Ivan, of course!'

'Oh, Ivan... In the bedroom—I *think* he's awake——' She was talking to empty air. When Katlin emerged from the bedroom talking flat out to her son, who was regarding her with a humorous air of puzzled resignation, Anne had coffee ready, which Katlin waved away.

'No, thanks, I've given up coffee. Makes me too jittery. I was drinking gallons of the stuff when the book wasn't going well.'

The past tense sounded promising. 'You mean it's going well now?'

Katlin looked at her over her son's head. Her smile was brilliant. She looked like the old, confident, exasperating Kat, supremely certain that the world revolved around her talent. 'Fantastically!'

Then, to Anne's bewilderment and Ivan's dismay, Katlin burst into tears.

CHAPTER EIGHT

KATLIN'S outburst of tears was as brief as it was violent. As she mopped her eyes, and those of Ivan, who had begun to wail in sympathy, she gave her sister a watery grin.

'Sorry. It's just seeing Ivan again. I didn't realise how much I'd miss him. I thought it'd be like ... I could just tuck him out of sight, out of mind for a while, but in the end I couldn't stand it so I borrowed the airfare off Don and just came. I mean, the writing's going great but ... you know, it was never *Ivan* that was the real problem, it was *me* and now I seem to have me all straightened out, well ... I guess what I'm trying to say is I don't want Ivan and me to be apart any longer.'

'You mean ... you want to move in here to write the rest of the book?' Anne asked when she got over her shock, feeling mean and petty because she wasn't whole-heartedly glad for her sister's sake.

'*God*, no!' Katlin shuddered. 'This city is so *claus-trophobic*. And I'm sure it's healthier for Ivan to grow up in a country environment. No, I want to take him back home with me. I've really got myself sorted out now, Anne, truly. It's all a matter of self-discipline, of setting realistic goals and not constantly doubting myself. I know I'm not anyone's notion of an ideal mother— even my own—but Ivan's part of my life now ... and I can't let him grow up thinking that I didn't want him.'

Kat's brown eyes softened as she kissed Ivan's downy cheek and she laughed as he blew a raspberry in response. 'We're going to be OK, aren't we, kiddo? I can't dance like Aunty Anne, but I can tell pretty good stories. If you like the ones I make up for you, maybe I could write them down and when you're bigger you can draw some pictures for them. Would you like that? We could call them *Ivan's Stories*. Maybe they could even get published one day!'

Ivan's fat cheeks creased and Katlin rubbed her nose against his, making him gurgle. 'Yes, they could... Maybe one day you'll be as famous as Christopher Robin.' She suddenly wrinkled her nose and sniffed. 'Or perhaps Pooh would be more appropriate—you need changing, my lad!'

Ivan's black eyes went wide as his mother whirled him around, laughing at her feeble pun. Anne didn't blame Ivan for being fascinated with this softer, more relaxed Katlin. More practical, too, as she asked where the nappies were kept and quickly completed the task, laughing at her own clumsiness and promising Ivan that she would improve with practice.

'So, what are you going to do about this place?' Anne asked shakily, trying not to sound as devastated as she felt.

'What?' Katlin blinked as she noticed her sister's pale face. 'Oh, Anne, you idiot, you're such a *worrier*!' Ivan was squeezed in between them as Katlin gave her a fierce hug. 'Of *course* I'm not going to chuck you out of here. After what you did for me? For heaven's sake, what do you think I am?'

At her sister's rueful face she laughed. 'No, don't answer that—I know I've been bloody selfish! But nothing's going to change for you, I promise, except you'll have to get by on a little less because I'll need more money for Ivan and me. In your letters you said you were earning a bit of money on the side, so you'll be OK, won't you?'

It was so unusual to have Katlin worrying about *her* that Anne smiled, mentally waving goodbye to the small savings account she had established for next year's fees.

'I can manage without any allowance at all if I don't have Ivan to work around,' she said firmly. 'I can get a proper part-time job. But don't you think it would be better just to come totally clean with the foundation?'

Katlin looked horrified. She hadn't changed *that* much. 'Oh, God, no, let's not rock the boat *now*, not while I've got this marvellous momentum going. I'll 'fess up later when it's all over, and don't worry, I promise I'll take all the blame. If they want the grant back...well, they can have my royalties. I don't care. At least I'll be *published*. Did I tell you that the publisher loved the partial?'

'No, that's terrific! It *must* be going well,' Anne murmured, reassured by the knowledge that it wasn't Katlin's ego alone talking.

'I told you it is!' Katlin brushed her favourite subject aside with startling impatience. 'But, talking of rocking boats, I'm not here *just* to pick up Ivan... I wonder if you could do one more little favour for me? Well, no, a really big, *big* favour, actually. But nothing dishonest or anything this time, I promise, just a bit awkward— but only for me...' she added hurriedly as she saw Anne's face tighten with apprehension.

She might have known that *nothing* Katlin asked for would be quite that simple...

'Look, really, Officer, I'm waiting here for a friend. I expect he'll be along any minute!'

To be mistaken for a prostitute by the police for the second time in the space of twenty-four hours was a bit much, thought Anne several hours later as she grimly hung on to her sense of humour.

She wasn't even dressed for the part. She had come straight from a late tutorial and her grey sweatshirt, white cotton trousers and flat black shoes were hardly provocative, but the fact that hardly an inch of flesh was on display didn't seem to deter the men who had approached her. The innocent, fresh-scrubbed look was obviously in big demand in ports around the world!

She glared at the small, wiry man who had got her into this trouble. She had thought he was helping her but they were evidently at cross-purposes because he had looked a picture of guilt when the wharf police had approached and asked to see their identification...

'He says he's not Dmitri,' the policeman was saying suspiciously.

'I *know* he's not Dmitri. I never said he was. I said I was asking him *about* Dmitri.'

Anne was glad that Katlin had finally come to the conclusion that she owed her lover the chance to acknowledge his son. The newspaper story about the Russian ship's return cruise to Auckland, on the verge of Katlin's own visit, had been an omen that her superstitious sister couldn't ignore, but Anne wished that she hadn't been the only intermediary that Katlin would trust!

Rather than contribute to her sister's apprehension by pointing out that it was quite possible that the man she had spent a single passionate week with had given her a false name, or was no longer on board the ship, or was merely a lowly seaman rather than the dashing officer he had made himself out to be, Anne had accepted the dog-eared photograph of the swarthy, handsome-looking man and agreed to try to see him and personally hand over a letter from Katlin. She was to note his reaction to the letter and carry a message back, if there was one, thus protecting Katlin from the trauma of a confrontation and possibly humiliating rejection.

Katlin was in her usual state of urgency. She had no intention of hanging around for days in an agony of uncertainty waiting for a written reply or a response to a shore-to-ship message that anyone might intercept or overhear. It all had to be settled *now*.

When she had arrived on the wharf Anne had noticed a number of well-dressed people arriving in cars and taxis, and had briefly toyed with the idea of trying to mingle with the crowd that was boarding the ship, but the visitors all seemed to have invitations which were being checked by the officer at the top of the gangplank.

The unhelpful sailor was now backing away, waving his arms and issuing a rapid stream of aggrieved Russian. Fortunately, from the blank look on the policeman's face, he understood even less than she did.

'Ah, there you are, Anne. What on earth are you doing here? I thought I told you to wait for me by the gate.'

Before Anne could react to Hunter's unexpected appearance she found herself grabbed and grimly kissed. When she was finally released, flushed and breathless, she found that the policeman had tactfully moved away.

Moments later she was being hustled up the gangplank.

'I can't do this!' she hissed at him, hurriedly stuffing the photo of Dmitri into her trouser pocket. 'I haven't been invited.'

'*I'm* inviting you,' he told her ominously, his voice as tight as the hand clamped around her elbow. Without breaking his stride he dug into the inner pocket of his dinner-jacket to flourish a gilt-edged card at the white-uniformed ship's officer who was inspecting the invitations.

Anne surreptitiously checked that the officer bore no resemblance to Dmitri's picture. She had wanted to get on board, but not like this. She had the feeling that Hunter intended to remain glued to her side.

'What happened, did your date for the evening let you down?' she asked acidly, remembering that he had left her to stew in uncertainty all day.

'I have some business to conduct. I didn't want the distraction. Besides, your baby-sitter told me you were going straight out from your evening tutorial.'

Anne stumbled on the smooth deck, forgetting her mingled annoyance and delight at being labelled a distraction. 'My baby-sitter?' she squeaked.

'The woman you had looking after Ivan today. Didn't she tell you I called in this afternoon between lectures?'

'No, she didn't,' Anne said weakly, acquitting Katlin of any deliberate malice. She had probably genuinely forgotten. Ivan, her book and Dmitri were her sole topics of interest at the moment. And to think that Anne had been on hot bricks all day wondering when her two worlds were going to collide, convinced that Hunter was regretting everything he had said and done the night before! 'What exactly did she say?'

'Not much. She seemed rather scatty and vague. Are you sure she's reliable?'

'Of course I'm sure!' Anne snapped, shuddering at the thought of the damage Katlin could have wrought if she *hadn't* been vague. But, after tonight, she hoped that there need be no more secrets between them.

'Hunter, I'm not dressed for anything posh. All the other women are in evening things.' The strong hand on her back continued to propel her along the deck. 'I'll make you look ridiculous!' she warned him desperately.

'You already have, twice in as many nights,' he warned back, but he turned sharply, pushing her through a brass-framed door into a narrow companionway. His black eyes quickly undressed her in the mellow yellow light.

'What have you got on under that sweatshirt?' he demanded.

Anne clamped a hand defensively to her breast. 'A leotard.'

'What colour?'

'Black.'

'Sexy? Low-cut?'

Her eyes narrowed angrily. 'None of your business.'

He fingered the bottom of her sweater meaningfully. 'I just made it my business.'

She slapped his hand away. 'All right, yes, it's low-cut. So what?'

'Take the sweater off.'

'What for?' She looked around incredulously. Surely he wasn't going to start anything *here*? She knew he was angry, but——

'Oh, for God's sake!' With swift impatience he forcibly stripped the sweater over her head, rolled it up ruthlessly small and stuffed it into her capacious black shoulder-bag. Then, while she was still spluttering, he spun her round and began pulling her hair out of its neat plait.

'What the——?'

When her hair was rippling down around her shoulders he spun her round again, hooked a finger in the low point of the sweetheart neckline of her shiny, sleeveless Lycra leotard and pulled it down another dramatic inch. Her cotton trousers had a high waist and pleats at the front which drew attention to the contrast between her trim hips and the generous curves above.

'Believe me, no one is going to notice that you're not in regulation evening wear,' he growled. 'Especially the men.'

'Well, it's not my fault,' she growled back, to hide her chagrin that his actions had been innocent of lust. 'I didn't ask to be hijacked out to sea.'

For a moment she thought he was going to smile but the gleam of appreciative humour must have been an illusion. 'We're not going anywhere,' he informed her tersely. 'The Russian Trade Commission is having a function on board to celebrate a new Russian-New Zealand tourism deal. Perhaps later you'll tell me what you were asking for down there on the dock. Or should I say *hustling* for...?'

'You know I wouldn't——'

'I really don't have time to go into it right now,' he cut her off abruptly, prodding her back towards the open deck. 'We're already late. You can explain everything later. For now just mind your manners and try to behave as if you're a *lady*...'

Hunter escorted her to a crowded bar and, suddenly warmly expansive, introduced her—in Russian—to the captain and several officers and various members of the Trade Commission who were impressed by her fledgling language skills. Anne glowed with pride and not even Hunter's amused condescension could dim her sense of accomplishment.

Unfortunately, nowhere did she see anyone who looked anything like Dmitri.

There was a light sprinkling of local celebrities but most of the guests appeared to be fairly anonymous and, apart from a few brief speeches when they moved into a small dining-room, there were few formalities. The main aim seemed to be for everyone to eat and drink themselves into a frivolous frame of mind and soon Anne had forgotten the uncomfortable circumstances of her arrival and was actually enjoying herself, in spite of the fact that Hunter would allow her only one small taste of iced vodka.

As she had feared, he also stuck close to her side and it was some time before she noticed that the only people they chatted to for any length of time were middle-aged men or couples, yet there were a number of unattached and personable young men present. Was Hunter being mistrustful or merely possessive? Anne wondered with slightly irritated amusement as he firmly steered her away from yet another engaging male grin. Another of his tricks was to brush a strand of hair back over her shoulder as she talked, the familiarity of the gesture a subtle male signal of protective interest that was silent but extremely effective.

'Am I forgiven?' he murmured in her ear as they finally rose after a superb dinner that had begun with caviare and *piroshki* and finished with *blinis*. Her pre-tutorial appetiser of macaroni cheese back at the flat hadn't stopped Anne from enjoying every splendid bite.

Now, with live Russian folk music playing in the background, there was apparently to be more vodka and vivacity and possibly a chance to escape Hunter's vigilance.

'What for?' she asked, aware that there was still a dangerous edge to his politeness, honed by undeniable success of his arrangement of her *décolletage*.

'Rescuing you from your own folly. You still haven't thanked me, by the way.'

'Thank you.' She owed him that, at the very least, although she couldn't resist the qualification, 'But it might be worth remembering that there are times when people might not want to be rescued from their folly.'

A brief, brooding shadow crossed his expression, then he acceded self-derisively, 'Quite so. I'll try to remember that the next time I'm tempted to play white knight.'

'You were more pirate than white knight,' Anne commented tartly.

'Once aboard the lugger and the girl is mine?' His black eyes gleamed at the hackneyed misquote. 'But the girl is mine already. It just remains to be seen how many others can make the same claim...'

'You already know there aren't any others,' she flared, unable to challenge his justifiable arrogance on any other grounds.

'All I know is what you choose to tell me,' he corrected her, pinning her with his flat black gaze. 'And sometimes you must admit that your words seem to be very much at odds with your actions...'

She wasn't listening. Over his shoulder Anne had seen a new face and all her attention was suddenly sharply focused on the other side of the room. Her hand went instinctively into her pocket and she fingered the creased photograph uneasily, wondering how on earth she was going to handle this with the discretion that Katlin had requested, particularly with Hunter in tow.

'I think I need another vodka.'

Unfortunately Hunter interpreted her response perfectly.

'Need or want, Anne? Either way I can tell you from bitter experience that Russian courage is no less tenuous than the Dutch variety.'

Her eyes snapped back to his face, afraid of what hers might have revealed. 'Did I *ask* for a psychoanalysis? I just want a drink!'

He studied her defensive expression thoughtfully for a moment and then said with disconcerting quietness, 'I'll get you one from the bar.'

'I'll just find somewhere to freshen up while you're getting it,' she gushed with relief, and made sure that his back was turned before she began wending her way across the crowded room.

He was wearing whites so he *was* an officer, and he must have just come off duty because he was making some kind of report to the captain. Anne waited until he appeared to have finished before catching the captain's eye and smiling prettily.

On cue he introduced her. 'Mr Fedorov is one of my senior officers. Dmitri, this is Miss Anne Tremaine. She is here with Hunter Lewis—from the Auckland university...'

Anne gravely shook hands with Ivan's father and they murmured a few polite banalities until the captain's attention was drawn by someone else. It seemed that Dmitri had also been waiting impatiently.

'Anne Tremaine,' he said in a low voice. 'You are Katlin's sister?'

Her eyes widened. 'How did you know?'

'She showed me a photograph of her family once. I only know that when we meet in Wellington she tells me she lives in the South Island. But you are here—can this be a coincidence?'

He spoke excellent English but his accent thickened with an eagerness that made Anne's dreaded task much easier.

'I'm living here in Auckland now, and Katlin is visiting me. I have a letter for you.' Anne felt for her bag, and handed it to him. He was older than he looked in the photograph, nearing forty, she guessed, the lines of experience on his face not detracting from his rugged handsomeness. 'It might be a bit of a shock.'

'Come. I will read it now.'

He was almost as forceful as Hunter, Anne thought wryly as she was steered outside on to the quiet deck. A few passengers were promenading, but most seemed to have gone ashore for their first night in a new port. Dmitri stood under a light and scanned the letter quickly. Anne could read nothing from his expression until he looked up and she saw his eyes. They were very bright and wondering, and instantly familiar. He was Ivan, looking out at a world filled with glorious possibilities.

'Where is she?'

In spite of the fact that she had instinctively liked him, Anne knew she should be cautious. Physically, Dmitri looked very strong. 'You're not angry that she waited this long?'

He smiled, his dark olive complexion warming. 'She wishes to see me. How can I be angry for that when I have wished it too? I will not hurt her, Anne, if that is your concern. You will take me to see Katlin—and my son. My patronym is Ivanovich, did she tell you that? Ivan was my father's name. So! We can leave now—yes?'

Anne shied away from his urgency. 'Oh, but——'

Dmitri pounced, hugging her, kissing her on both cheeks with laughing exuberance. 'Oh, but you must, little sister; that is what you are here for—the letter says so! You must take me home with you...I am off duty until tomorrow afternoon so I have all the long night...'

Anne couldn't help laughing at his earnest enthusiasm. She had the feeling that once they got to the flat he would be just as eager to get rid of her. 'But I'm with someone——'

'The lady means me.'

The quiet phrase, spoken with silken menace, sliced them apart. They both swung around and Anne groaned inwardly.

Hunter stood just outside the encircling pool of light, his shadowy form managing to exude even more menace than his voice.

'Aren't you going to introduce us, Anne?' He moved into the light, holding out her drink in a travesty of politeness. His eyes were deeply hooded, his mouth a square gash in a lantern jaw.

Anne took the cold glass because she didn't know quite what else to do. She stammered a bald introduction and on hearing Dmitri's name Hunter's expression grew even icier.

He said something, harshly, in rattling Russian, to Dmitri, who replied in contrasting quiet, even tones that Anne followed easily, 'She is taking me to meet my son... and perhaps my fate...'

It said everything and yet Hunter, in his ignorance, misunderstood. Anne touched him on the arm. 'Hunter, please—— '

His muscles were like rigid steel as he shook her off as if her touch revolted him. 'You came here to meet him?'

The clipped question gave her no room to manoeuvre. 'Well, yes, but it's not what you think——'

'He's not Ivan's father? You're not going to leave with him?' His eyes were smouldering with outrage at the realisation that she had merely used him to get to another man.

'Well, yes, but——'

He said something under his breath. 'My God, no wonder you were so shocked to see me on the wharf. Did I wreck a secret rendezvous? Why all the furtiveness? Is he already married?'

Anne sent Dmitri a faltering look. The last of the peppered questions was one that she had meant to ask but had quite overlooked in her relief at finding him.

'No, Anne, I am not married,' he said, his faint amusement at her uncertainty having a deleterious effect on Hunter's finely balanced temper. 'I am very free and available.'

'You're really going to trust his word on that? You don't trust me——' Hunter turned on Anne furiously '—and you know a hell of a lot more about me than you apparently do about roving lover-boy here. Why don't you ask him how many other bastards he's fathered in his wake——?'

'I have done nothing to be ashamed of!' Dmitri was as proud as his grim opponent and Anne was alarmed to see his fists bunch at his sides at the blatant insult to his honour. 'I had no knowledge of the child. It was not *my* choice to lose touch. I was in love with her——'

Both men were squaring off and, afraid that there was going to be a fight right there on the deck, Anne rushed to defuse the tension. 'He's right—Hunter, please, you've got it all wrong. Why don't you come back to the flat with us?'

Hunter's head swung around heavily and he looked at her incredulously, his voice clotted with angry disbelief. 'No, thanks, I told you I was a conservative. A *ménage à trois* is just not my scene.'

Anne blocked a sharply aggressive move from Dmitri. 'It wouldn't be that,' she persisted doggedly.

'What if I asked you to choose? Him or me?'

She was so taken aback by the absurdity of the demand that she hesitated, only for a heartbeat but it was an eternity too long.

'Quite.' Hunter slid the verbal knife into the momentary silence and made the slashing excision. 'That choice was made, wasn't it, Anne, as soon as you set eyes on him? After that I was just an inconvenience to be got rid of.' He blistered a sardonic look at the forgotten drink clutched in Anne's hand. 'I needn't have worried about compromising your independence—you're evidently more than capable of ruthless self-interest.' He made her a faint, mocking bow. 'I won't be hypocrite enough to wish you both a pleasant evening. In point of fact, I hope you both rot in hell!'

Anne was stiff with shock as she watched him go, every long stride managing to express a searing contempt for those he left behind, or, more specifically, her.

'Do you want to go after him and explain?' Dmitri asked with discouraging impatience. It was obvious what he hoped her answer would be. 'He does seem confused about you and Katlin...'

That was such a masterly understatement that Anne almost smiled. She closed her eyes and sighed wearily. It had been a trauma-filled twenty-four hours and now, it seemed, there were still more rough waters ahead.

'Somehow I don't think it would do much good in the mood he's in, even if I could find him . . . Hunter's had a lot of practice at being elusive.'

She opened her eyes and met Dmitri's frowning gaze. 'I'm sure I can clear it up quietly with him later. Make it right with him,' she added firmly, when it appeared that the slang was alien to interpretation.

He must have perceived the despair underlying her steadfast optimism. 'He was angry to see you with another man. He means a lot to you, I can see that. Go. I have waited this long to see Katlin again, I can wait a little longer . . .'

They had a brief argument but Anne's practicality won over Dmitri's forced gallantry. As she pointed out, she had plenty of time to pound sense into Hunter's hard head, while Dmitri's ship was due to sail in three days' time.

Dmitri had to clear his absence with the duty officer, and while he went briefly down to his quarters Anne waited by the top of the boarding steps, refusing to risk the possibility of running into Hunter again and facing down his hostility in public. He had been jealous. She held the knowledge to her bruised heart. He had not just been angry; there had been a deeper thread of emotion that had added to his bitterness, his disappointment at what he perceived to be a betrayal. He had believed her loyalty was due to him. He had been prepared to protect her, to fight for her. She had yet to be allowed to prove that she was prepared to do the same for him.

As she had wryly presumed, she was somewhat superfluous to requirements once Dmitri had been introduced to a snoozing Ivan and the awkward conversation between the two ex-lovers began to limp uncomfortably towards a kind of reconciliation. At first Katlin, wary and defensive, wouldn't let her go to bed, and Dmitri too seemed to prefer to channel his questions and answers through a third party, but after a few cups of coffee and a growing, irritable awareness of how they were tiptoeing around the central issue Anne took herself off with the firm opinion that she was not cut out to be Cupid. It was up to Katlin and Dmitri to sort themselves out.

She lay awake for hours listening to the indistinct murmurs in the other room, pretending to herself that she was anxious for her sister when really she was waiting for the familiar bumps and rustles of movement that signalled Hunter going to bed. When they came at last it was nearly two in the morning by Anne's luminous watch dial and there were a lot more thumps and stumbles than usual, and a string of ragged curses that indicated a less than sober occupant of the bed next door. She turned on her stomach and put a hand against the wall, pressing hard so that she could feel the vibration caused by his tossing and turning. Finally she could stand it no more. She crouched up and cupped her hand around her mouth, sealing it to the wall so that her visitors, and Ivan, bubbling sweetly in the corner, wouldn't hear.

'Hunter?'

The restless nudging of his bed against the wall stopped.

'Hunter?'

Utter stillness and silence. Shivering in the warm night air, Anne crawled back under her thin sheet, tears stinging her eyes. She had never felt lonely before she'd come to the city. She had never felt real isolation until she had met Hunter. Whoever said that war, hunting and love had a thousand pains for one pleasure was right... only she hadn't even been granted the one pleasure yet!

She bunched the sheet around her face to muffle a sniff, and then another.

'Go to sleep.'

The slurred directive brought her head sharply up from the pillow. 'Hunter?'

'I said go to sleep, dammit!'

It was a snarl, but quite a nice one as snarls went, Anne decided as she snuggled down again, the hollow feeling in her chest easing. At least he was prepared to acknowledge that she was still alive. She sniffed again, just to let him know that she wasn't totally cowed, and there was a corresponding growl that degenerated into a drowsy rumble. Her eyes closed and the gentle rumble continued and she smiled. He was snoring. It was something to tease him with and, God knew, she would need every advantage she could rake up to handle their next encounter.

Ivan woke her out of a deep sleep at six and she staggered out to the living-room, bleary-eyed, to find Katlin and Dmitri holding hands on the couch, still talking, their voices as rusty as old cans. While Dmitri played with his son, Katlin followed Anne into the kitchenette and, while she started getting breakfast for them all, told her some of the plans that the two of them had made in the night. Anne was vastly relieved to discover that none of them included her.

Dmitri was due some leave and he thought that he could take it immediately on compassionate grounds, by pleading that he wanted to spend some time with his newly discovered New Zealand son, and rejoin his ship in Sydney in a fortnight's time. If that could be done, he and Katlin would go back to Golden Bay together, to sort out what they wanted to do long-term and so that

Dmitri could begin to learn to know his son, although he was already talking about applying for residency and building a new life for himself in the peaceful, evergreen country he had so admired on his last visit.

On a more practical note, he had pointed out that he could help care for his son, so that Katlin could have the bonus of a little more writing time.

'I'm not just using him either, if that's what you think,' murmured Katlin when Dmitri was occupied with Ivan. 'It was never just the casual fling I pretended it was. He was my first, you see, and it's a pretty traumatic thing to give your virginity away at my age. I just panicked when Dmitri started getting too intense and I didn't know how to handle it so I scuttled home... and then when I found I was pregnant...! I really didn't think there was room in my life for anyone... Maybe Dmitri will be able to show me differently. I hope so. He's nice, isn't he...?'

He looked even nicer when he returned in jeans and a sweater, carrying his captain's permission and—as indication of his sincerity as well as his efficiency—a sheaf of immigration forms and leaflets.

Meanwhile Katlin had checked flights and frantically tossed out most of her clothing from her old battered suitcase and crammed in Ivan's, parcelled up his toys in a large plastic shopping bag and folded up and secured his port-a-cot and high chair in a tight bundle.

An hour after that Anne was alone and wondering what had hit her. The hollow feeling had returned with a vengeance and so had the self-pitying tears. Trailing back up the stairs after waving the taxi off to the airport, she could hardly see where she was going, so it was not surprising that she walked into the solid wall of muscle hovering outside her door.

'My God, what's happened? That worthless bastard's run out on you again, hasn't he? I told you not to trust him. And now I suppose you expect me to pick up the pieces!'

CHAPTER NINE

'I HOPE you used some form of protection this time.'

Anne froze in the act of handing back the snowy white handkerchief, now crumpled and damp. She must look a mess—a headache from her tears and lack of sleep, her hair in a half-hearted ponytail, her nose pink and shiny as it always was when she cried, her swirling floral print skirt bunched up around her legs where Hunter had plonked her on the couch after literally carrying her into the flat.

'I beg your pardon?' she wavered, unnerved by the ferocious expression on his face, the waves of silent anger she could feel beating the air between them as he crouched down in front of her, his eyes glittering with some fiercely repressed emotion. She noticed with a detached part of her brain that those black eyes were definitely bloodshot, his hair was uncombed and his denim shirt only half tucked into his jeans. All in all he had the aura of a man who was distinctly frayed around the edges.

'There's a vital difference between sexual liberation and sexual irresponsibility,' he told her forbiddingly. 'You were lucky with Ivan. You have the support of your family and the talent and drive to make something of yourself in spite of the handicaps of solo parenthood.' He plucked the used handkerchief from her astonished hand and tossed it aside as he frowned critically at her.

'Maybe that's the problem. Maybe you've been *too* insulated from the consequences of your actions to realise the risks you're taking. Reckless behaviour doesn't just lead to accidental pregnancy... For God's sake,

Anne, indiscriminate sex can also be a sentence of *death*. And don't look so shocked,' he added roughly. 'I'm not talking about *you*, I'm talking about *him*.'

He jerked to his feet and began pacing up and down in front of her. Anne, whose jaw had dropped open when she'd realised she was being delivered a stern lecture on sexual responsibility, closed it with an audible click as Hunter abruptly veered from his tone of strained reason to one of unrestrained fury.

'What in hell were you thinking of? You're supposed to be a bloody intelligent woman, yet you acted like a gullible sixteen-year-old. Even if he convinced you that you were still in love with him, how could you let a guy whom you haven't seen for over a year—during which he's been doing God knows what with God knows whom—talk his way into your bed on the strength of a few hours' reacquaintance? Surely you didn't fall for that line about fate? I saw the way he looked at you and, believe me, it wasn't the way a man looks at a woman he's in love with——'

'That's because he was never in love with *me*,' said Anne, shaking off her dumb shock in the soaring knowledge that she was finally free to confide in him.

He halted in front of her, hands on hips, voice dripping with ice. 'You know that and you still let him make you so desperate for human comfort that when he crawled into your bed you *welcomed* him——?'

'Of course I didn't!' Anne yelped at him, as outraged as he by the notion.

'The hell you didn't!' he stormed, the ice turning to fire. 'Don't lie, on top of everything else. I'm not *stupid*. I saw him leaving this morning—he was here all night, wasn't he?'

He didn't wait for her answer. 'Whatever you thought I did to you, I didn't deserve that.' His tone became savage. 'Was he lying there beside you when you made that touching little plea through the wall? Were you both snivelling with laughter at the thought of having driven me to drown my sorrows like some pathetic bloody caricature of rejection——?' His face was a mask of loathing as he vomited out the humiliating vision of himself as the drunken butt of their sly jokes.

'*No*! No, I would never do a thing like that to you, Hunter, *never*. And certainly not with Dmitri! He didn't sleep with me last night because it wasn't even me he came to see——'

'I suppose he's told you he wants Ivan,' he interrupted harshly. 'He knows all the right buttons to push, doesn't he? He probably realises that you'd do anything for your son. He's manipulating you, can't you see that?' Hunter clenched his teeth and drew a savagely controlling breath, briefly bowing his head as he visibly struggled to master his emotions. 'Where is he, by the way?' he asked in a voice taut with the effort.

'Dmitri?'

He flared up at the conjured image. 'No! *Ivan*.'

Anne looked around her strangely empty flat. No nappies airing, no scattered baby paraphernalia, no toothy grin and fearsomely questing button-black eyes. No one to listen to her daily delights and devastations, to light her life with his innocence and joy, a world away from adult woes.

She swallowed, hard. 'He's gone.'

'Gone?' He looked at her with puzzled impatience. 'Gone where?'

'Home.' Anne looked at her hands, foolishly close to tears again. It was so silly. It wasn't as if she'd never see Ivan again. She was still his aunt . . . his favourite, only aunt. Whatever happened in her life Ivan would always have a special place in her heart. And for all she knew the grand plans with Dmitri would founder on the rocks of reality and Katlin would be back in a couple of weeks' time pleading for her to take her nephew again.

'Anne?' She refused to look at him in the ensuing thunderstruck silence and he sat down on the over-stuffed couch and lifted her jaw with his hand, his thumb roughly underscoring her brimming left eye. 'What do you mean, gone home?' he demanded roughly. 'His home is here with you.' He swore. 'My God, you couldn't have let that bastard persuade you that you weren't a fit mother.'

'But I'm not——'

'Don't!' His fingers tightened, pinching her jaw closed as he ordered thickly, 'Don't you ever say that. You bore him in your body, you suckle him at your breast, you love him, lavish him with care...' He stroked her cheek with the knuckles of his other hand. 'A more perfect mother I can't imagine...'

'But I *didn't* do all those things,' she whispered, half hypnotised by the fathomless black eyes, wondering whether the tenderly knowing touch would turn brutal at the moment of truth. She put her hands over his and eased them away from her face, clasping them unconsciously to her heart. 'I mean, yes, I love him, but he's not mine. He never was.' She took a deep breath and twined her fingers in his. 'Ivan's my nephew, not my son.'

Not by the flicker of an eyelash did Hunter show any reaction to her earth-shattering revelation.

Anne cleared her throat anxiously, certain that his un-natural stillness was a bad sign.

'I've been looking after him for my sister who's been very ill and depressed since his birth... Her home is pretty isolated and we were all very worried about her. The book was going badly and...well...when she begged me to bring Ivan up here with me I couldn't say no. But then yesterday she just turned up out of the blue saying she missed him and wanted him back... You even met her—the "scatty" baby-sitter? That was my big sister.'

The feeble attempted at levity withered under his fixed gaze.

Her nerves tightened another notch and she had to moisten her dry lips before she could continue. 'She's not really scatty, she just comes across that way sometimes. I mean, she was certainly efficient enough to get herself and Dmitri and Ivan skipped up the waiting-list on to a flight to Nelson today. That's where they've gone—so that Dmitri can meet Mum and Dad and spend a few weeks at Golden Bay to see . . . well, to see how he might fit in if that was the way things could be worked out . . .

'I offered to go too.' She waved her arm vaguely to indicate that she meant away from the flat and continued, even more incoherently, 'But they said I should stay and see things through. I mean, there's still the book to finish and the conditions of the grant to meet so I suppose I can't really let them down . . .' Her voice nearly failed her but she forced herself to say earnestly, 'I'm sorry for deceiving you but when we started out I just thought it would make things less complicated if I let people assume that Ivan was mine——'

'Assume? *Assume*?' For a moment her fingers were trapped in a bone-crushing grip, then they were tossed violently into her lap. 'And tell me, then, did I just *assume* that you were breast-feeding?'

She blushed brilliantly, her trembling hands twisting and turning in her lap. 'I—I don't know why I said that. It just sort of came out on the spur of the moment. I— Ivan is a bottle-baby, of course, because my sister was too ill to feed him. Really, she had a very bad time of it and there was no one else in the family who could take him . . . My mother's back isn't up to much lifting and Ivan is such a solid baby . . .'

Anne was aware that she was beginning to babble but she couldn't help it; she had to get it all out before Hunter exploded. She could read the signs—the dangerously hooded eyes, the building colour, the small tic at the corner of his compressed mouth.

'It was something I had to do, Hunter, for my sister's sake as well as Ivan's. Surely you can understand that? He's such a darling boy, he deserves the best start possible for his life. And I didn't mind; I loved him... I didn't know that things were going to get so *complicated*...'

As a plea for sympathy her bewildered wail fell on stony ground.

'And Dmitri? What part does lover-boy play in all this?' he asked ominously.

'None! At least not as far as I'm concerned,' she assured him hastily. 'They'd split up... Until last night he never even knew he had a son. So that's what I was doing down at the ship, acting as a sort of go-between in case he reacted badly——'

It was the match to his fuse. 'So as usual you were the one taking all the risks? Why in *hell* didn't you tell me this last night?' he roared.

'Because it wasn't my story to tell!' she jumped up to inform him at equal volume, prepared to fight a desperate rear-guard action. Her happiness depended on it.

'You were willing to give your body to me but not your trust, is that it? How much longer did you intend to keep me in the dark? Weeks? *Months*? Were you *ever* going to trust me, or was I just not important enough to bother?' He towered fiercely over her. 'And now— now that your family plot's been unexpectedly tied up in this nice, tidy bundle, *now* you insult me with my own gullibility.'

She'd been afraid he would think that. 'I wasn't trying to make a fool of you, Hunter,' she said gently.

'Perhaps you weren't but you managed to succeed magnificently all the same.' He raked his hand through his hair and gave a bitterly unamused laugh. 'My God, Anne, have you *any* idea what you've put me through?'

'A *very* good idea,' she said wryly, thinking of her own agonies of doubt.

Their eyes met in a moment of brief accord and for that moment Anne felt almost a part of him, feeling what he felt, knowing what he knew.

Lulled by the false promise of his momentary tranquillity, she smiled slowly, the tender dimple in her left cheek winking at him, innocently provocative. A second later she squeaked in dismay as she was snatched off her feet and suspended by her slim shoulders from two powerful hands.

'You're damned lucky I'm not a violent man!'

He didn't seem to see any irony in the remark and this time Anne didn't make the mistake of taking it lightly. She tilted her head back, exposing her throat in an instinctive act of mock-submission, knowing that if he wanted to he could hurt her badly.

'You *lied* to me.'

She held her chin up. 'Well, yes, but there were extenuating circum——'

He wasn't interested in explanations. 'So you have no son?' He gave her a little shake to prise an immediate answer loose. 'No Russian lover?'

She shook her head to both, wondering apprehensively where he was leading as his grip eased and her toes brushed the floor.

'No husband?'

'No!'

'No daughter?'

'*No*!' She clutched at his thick forearms, wobbling slightly as he let her legs take her full weight and she discovered that her knees were unusually weak.

'Just making sure,' he said grimly, shifting a splayed hand to her back, applying just enough pressure to bring the tips of her breasts against his denim shirt. 'In your case it pays to be explicit. So there are no other skeletons likely to shamble out of your closet?'

She began to struggle, detecting a menacing new element in his quiet interrogation. 'No! Dammit, Hunter, stop trying to frighten me. I know you're not going to hurt me. Let me go.'

The heat of his body was producing a musky aroma that prompted a pulse of startled recognition along her senses. She faltered, briefly tempted, then pride came to her rescue and she renewed her struggles. But her supple strength was no match for his resolute toughness and he controlled her with irritating ease, the brazen pressure of his thighs confirming her sizzling suspicions. She could feel herself getting hot and flustered as she twisted and turned, unable to escape the knowledge that her efforts were achieving the opposite to what she intended. Her temper rose in direct proportion to her helplessness. 'I said—let—me—go!'

'Why?' he murmured tauntingly down into her flushed, antagonistic face. 'There's no one waiting for you—you've been deserted by your nearest and dearest, remember? You're quite, quite alone—except for me, of course...'

The hand on her right shoulder moved clumsily, snagging in her soft collar and dragging the open neck of her flowing blouse diagonally down across her shoulder until the top button popped.

'Now look what you've done! You've pulled the button off,' she accused, grabbing at the opportunity to make *him* feel guilty for a change. His eyelids drooped and she realised with a thrill of consternation that his clumsiness hadn't been accidental.

'How dare you?' she said weakly, trying to disguise her delicious ambivalence.

His smile was slow, predatory, prematurely triumphant. 'Good cliché, bad defence, darling. What's next? You *could* claim it's feeding time, but no, that excuse won't work any more for you, will it? There's no one left here for you to feed...unless it's me...'

With stunning arrogance his hand moved down, cupping her breasts, fondling them through the soft, well-washed cotton as he murmured with a sexual frankness calculated to shock, 'I thought these were swollen with milk for your baby... I'm delighted to find out that they're always this large and luscious—like lovely, warm, ripe fruit just begging to be plucked and tasted...'

And on that insolent note his finger ran lightly down into her cleavage to hook under the next button. Anne gave a gasping cry as with a casual downward flick of his powerful wrist he ripped the rest of her blouse open from collarbone to waist.

Buttons scattered, along with most of Anne's remaining resistance. If he was deliberately trying to shame her she wasn't going to co-operate by fighting him, and if it was violent seduction he had in mind then she was a more than willing victim. Her love was stronger than her pride and because of that she could give him the plea that she sensed his own pride demanded. She placed her hands on his shoulders, tacitly opening herself to his touch.

'Hunter, please...'

'That's what you said last time, and I did please you, didn't I?' He peeled back the edges of her blouse, displaying her soft, filmy bra, and bent his head to nip at the dark, rosy centres pressed flat against the creamy net. 'Now it's your turn to please me...'

He opened his mouth against her and she went utterly weak, not even noticing the rough hand glide smoothly under her hanging blouse and unclip the plastic fastening at her back. As her breasts tumbled free he made a rough sound of greedy satisfaction and sank back down with her on to the firmly sprung couch, holding her across his lap and nuzzling the flimsy fabric aside with his mouth before lapping at the soft, shyly trembling peaks with long, lazy strokes, gliding them with his clever tongue until they were rigid and glistening. He admired

his erotic creations with little crowns of biting kisses,
then cupped her again in his strong fingers, guiding each
stiff nipple in turn into the scalding moistness of his
mouth, drawing them deeper as he suckled hotly, with
a fierce, lusty enjoyment that drove her into a frenzy of
delight.

Fiery needles lanced through Anne's flesh, concentrating their piercing sensations on the pleasure centres
of her body as Hunter shifted sideways and rolled deftly
over, pushing her full-length on to the soft, polished-
cotton cushions and coming down heavily on top of her,
using his hips to wedge her thighs open and accept him
as intimately as their clothing would allow.

Anne was lost in a world of languid bliss, unaware of
the passage of time as Hunter teased her skirt slowly up
her legs, deliberately taking his time in order to savour
her uninhibitedly sensual response to each fleeting caress,
his warm fingers stroking, delving, sliding, enticing, his
mouth always moving, tasting, exploring her with a
thoroughness that would have shocked her had she not
been blinded by the shattering glory of her first physical
experience of love.

She wasn't aware of the skilful disrobing that accompanied his wildly erotic explorations until she opened
her pleasure-dazed eyes and suddenly found herself nude
in her lover's arms, unbearably excited by the feel of his
rough clothing against her singing skin, the slide of
smooth cotton against her bare back as he shifted her
to accommodate his needs. He had released her hair from
its faded hoop of elastic and fanned it out to frame the
lush, pearly curves of her body, winding his hands in its
gleaming luxuriance, teasing it over her gloriously sen-
sitised breasts, tantalising her with its feathery friction.

When she teased him throatily about his fetish and
protested at the inequity of their dress, Hunter laughed
smokily and touched her where she was most vulnerable, stroking her with excruciating delicacy until she

melted with a drenching cry, praising her for the splendour of her response.

'So soft, and hot and silky wet... Don't lose the rhythm, darling, stay with me... that's right... a little harder... a little faster... No, darling, don't fight it...'

Each time she tried to do so, out of fear or innate modesty, he punished her with a new, even more irresistible form of ravishment. With exquisite finesse he drew her deeper and deeper into unknown territory, closer and closer to the secret source of the molten river of hedonistic pleasure, yet never quite allowing her to achieve enlightenment, tantalising her with the certain knowledge that she would only find it with him...

And when she couldn't bear to wait any longer, and tore impatiently at the cloth which veiled the ultimate mystery from her, he was too fiercely in the grip of his own pulsing arousal to continue the bewitching game, stripping to the skin with shaking hands and guiding her fingers as he prepared himself to take her, fumbling like an inexperienced boy with the tiny packet and groaning as she tentatively stroked the length of his satiny hardness, his big body arching and shuddering with the same rippling tension that she could feel building inside her, his taut buttocks and powerful flanks flexing with an inexorable rhythm as he pushed himself helplessly against her soft palm.

He caught her wrist and dragged it urgently away. 'Stop it, or I'll...'

He moaned, shivering convulsively as she enclosed him with her free hand, bolder now, unable to resist her new fascination with his smooth shape and daunting size, the way he pulsed heavily against her fingers.

'Or you'll what?' she dared to tease.

'Or I'll do this!'

It happened so quickly she had no time to warn him. He was parting her, then sliding sleekly inside with a thick, sensual growl of gratification as she closed tightly

around his swollen hardness. To her dazed delight there
was no pain...he had been too skilled, too intent in
indulging his evident preference for extensive love-play.

'It doesn't hurt,' she sighed with revealing eagerness,
arching beneath him to rub her breasts against the dense,
dark, silky hair of his chest.

He caught his breath, rising up on bulging arms, his
hips pressing deeper, tighter as her body absorbed and
adjusted itself to him in minute increments. 'No lover,
Anne? Or no lovers *at all*?' he murmured raggedly.

Anne let her head fall back. Even at a critical moment
like this the man was full of wretched curiosity!

'Who cares now...?' She moaned and clutched desperately at him as he suddenly withdrew, but it was only
to slide forward again, sheathing himself even more
deeply this time, his breathing harshening as the tension
shivered across his hard belly and a sheen of sweat began
to glisten on his thickly muscled shoulders and in his
tangled chest-hair.

He braced his knees against the firm springs, his feet
against the high-rolled arm of the couch, blessing the
fact that it was a trifle too short for a man of his size
as he used the resulting leverage to control carefully the
instinctive aggression of his thrusts, drawing another
wondrously flattering sigh from the new-born voluptuary beneath him.

'Am I the first man to do this to you, Anne?'

He withdrew once more, and again she couldn't stop
herself from panicking, digging her short, practical nails
into his tight buttocks until he eased forward, this time
a little faster and more roughly, beginning to establish
a rhythm that was both exhilarating and frustrating.

'Am I, Anne?'

This time as he pulled back Hunter deliberately hesitated and, as he expected, his answer arrived in a wild
rush as she wound herself around him.

'Yes, yes! Although if I'd known it was going to be *this* good I wouldn't have waited so long!' She slid her fingers through the hair on his chest and stroked the fine pelt, following the silky line down his belly to push into the thickening where his body joined with hers—Anne and Hunter, Hunter and Anne—if only it could go on forever. 'Oh, what does it *matter*? What does *anything* matter? Just shut up, Hunter, and keep doing whatever it is you're doing and, whatever happens, this time *don't stop*!'

There was a quiver of laughter in his voice as he responded explosively to her desperate order. 'Don't worry, little tyrant, there's no danger of that. Hold on tight, now—I have a feeling this is going to be a turbulent ride!'

Anne lay on her back in a state of blissful exhaustion, staring at the afternoon sunlight painting patterns on the white ceiling of her bedroom.

'So that's what all the fuss is about!' she said smugly to the sweat-soaked man lying beside her.

'I take it you're quite satisfied?' Hunter smiled at her gloating expression, rising on one elbow to regard her sprawling figure.

'Didn't I give that vague impression?' she said lightly, although secretly she was embarrassed. She knew she had amused him with her effervescent enthusiasm.

It was too much to expect that he wouldn't guess. 'You're a very passionate woman; don't apologise for it.'

'Is that what I was doing?' She suddenly realised that the sheets were twisted underneath her and she sat up, trying to tussle the top one free to cover her nakedness.

Hunter took the sheet out of her hand and threw it out of reach on the floor. Then he lay back and stretched, long and luxuriously, in an unnecessarily flagrant display of his rippling physique. Still, his ease with his nudity made her less self-conscious about her own.

She frowned at him. 'I might have been cold,' she said haughtily.

He smiled at her lazily. 'You might have been. But you weren't. Aren't you going to ask how I know?'

His eyes drifted down to her breasts and she instinctively raised her hands to shield her soft nipples from his provocative glance, flushing as she felt them pucker lightly in loving memory.

He chuckled. She had never seen him so mellow and relaxed, totally at peace with the world and, she realised with a quickening of her pulse, with her. Yet even at his most passionate he had maintained an emotional distance that had precluded words of love in his love-making vocabulary... as if they were still, in his mind, reserved for someone else. For Deborah, she thought sinkingly. The serious wife his mother had disapproved of, but whom he had evidently loved enough to make him shy away from committing himself to anyone else.

'Are you always like this after sex?' she asked him jealously. If he didn't use love-words, neither would she.

He raised his eyebrows, his expression cooling. 'It depends on whether I enjoyed it or not.'

She tossed her head at the non-answer, and a swath of long hair flicked across his chest, catching against the curly thatch and pulling at it slightly as she whisked it away again, causing him to suck in his stomach with a small shudder.

'Remind me to get you to do that to me properly some time,' he murmured huskily.

'What?'

'Stroke me with your hair.'

The now familiar weakness invaded her belly with a warm tingling. 'You're not going to answer my question, are you?' she made herself ask.

He studied her stubborn face for a moment. 'No, I'm not. I consider it intrusive and an invasion of privacy.'

She paled as if she had been slapped, turning her head sharply aside so that she didn't notice his hand beginning to lift in a brief gesture of conciliation, then dropping back to his side.

'Anne, we're two mature adults with separate pasts and personalities and a way of life that demands a great deal of personal space,' he said quietly. 'I don't like being crowded and neither, if today's events are anything to go by, do you. We've both made mistakes but only because we were impatient for this...' He splayed his hand between them on the bed, his tone drifting into detached 'lecturer' mode that made her long to shake him. 'If we're going to be lovers we have to set the boundaries of mutual consideration, so that neither of us develops unreal expectations of the other. This business with Ivan is an illustration in point. There are obviously areas of your life in which you want to keep your own counsel and make your own decisions without my advice or interference and I respect that. In turn you need to respect my need for the same kind of personal privacy. It doesn't mean we can't ask questions, only that we shouldn't be offended if the answer is not the one we want it to be. Just because we're lovers it doesn't mean that we have to turn each other inside out...'

'I rather thought that was just what we *had* done,' said Anne, recovering her sense of humour and giving him a pert grin.

'Lovers'. That was what he had called them. Not sex partners or friends. 'Lovers'. It had a lovely, warm, semi-permanent kind of sound to it. Some people were lovers for years, for decades, for the rest of their natural lives...

He responded with a rakish answering smile but his words were cautious. 'You may be right. So we're agreed, then—no encroachment, no tantrums——'

'I'm not the one who had the big tantrum,' she pointed out.

'Mmm.' His eyes narrowed resentfully. He didn't like being reminded of it. 'Acquit me on this occasion because personal privacy does *not* include the right to take other lovers, let alone flaunt them under my nose. I'm not *that* liberated and I never will be!'

He swung abruptly off the bed and began picking up his clothes, his movements masking his expression.

'So I'm allowed to be jealous, then?' said Anne a trifle snippily, thinking that he didn't seem to notice that, for all his obsession with mutual benefits, *he* was the one setting all the rules.

At least he hadn't ordered her not to fall in love with him—she had broken that one already! 'I have permission to run off any strange blondes who might follow you home?'

His mouth twitched and he turned, clothes in hand, to fluster her with another full-frontal. 'By all means. I like you when you're fierce, stroking me with that sharp little tongue, especially as it lies in such a delectable sheath.'

He confirmed his approval by leaning over and kissing her, delicately stroking the tongue in question with his own. 'Mind if I use your shower before I go?' He didn't wait for an answer, sauntering out with a long, easy stride that in a younger man might have been mistaken for a self-satisfied swagger.

He was gone so long that Anne took fright, thinking that he might have left without bothering to say goodbye, or that he had merely been some grief-induced hallucination. She hurriedly pulled on her modest robe and scuttled out, coming to a skidding stop on the wooden floor.

She might have known!

Showered but unshaven, Hunter was sitting in his jeans and shirt at her small desk, reading Katlin's manuscript. At least, he was holding it—but he was actually staring at the painting on the wall directly across from him with a brooding expression that made her nervous.

'Er...your mother absolutely *insisted* I have it,' she began uneasily.

'Where's the rest of it?'

Anne was bewildered. 'What do you mean? That's all there is.'

'Three chapters?'

He was talking about the book! 'Oh, *that*——'

'Yes, that.' He held the sheaf of papers out to her. 'This is exactly what was submitted to the awards committee, no more, no less. Not even any revisions. You don't seem to have written a single usable line since you've been here.' He threw the manuscript down on the desk where it drifted in the mess of university papers. 'There's nothing here, not even a draft of your next few chapters. Well, from now on you're just going to have to get your head down and finish it.'

'*Me*?' she squeaked.

He frowned at her inanity. 'I certainly don't see anyone else in the room,' he said in the acid tones for which he was famous.

She gaped at him. 'Hunter, what are you *talking* about?'

'I'm *talking* about the fact that I believe you have a brilliant career ahead of you if you can only learn to discipline your talent. I'm talking about the people who've put their trust in that talent. You owe it to them to finish this. You owe it to *me*, dammit! I'm not going to be trotted out as another excuse for your procrastination and I certainly don't want Arnold Markham on my back accusing me of sabotaging one of his cherished protégées...'

'You know Arnold Markham...*personally*?' Anne gulped, wiping her sweating palms against her robe, feeling dizzy as she racked her brains as to why on earth

Hunter was still going on at her as if she were the Markham prize-winner.

Hadn't she taken her courage in her hands and bared her entire soul to him? Hadn't she just explained all about Kat and her illness and how she had begged Anne to take her place and look after Ivan while she finished the book? Hadn't he just forgiven her all her sins by making beautiful love to her?

Or had she simply been too preoccupied with appeasing his rage as quickly as possible to put the facts clearly in a logical progression?

Anne felt suddenly faint. Just what *had* she confessed to? In her confused jumble of thoughts she had assumed that somewhere in her stumbling phrases she had dealt with the basic matter of identity. She back-tracked desperately over the stops and starts and twists and turns of their emotional conversation. Had she even mentioned Katlin's *name* in her headlong rush to absolve herself? Oh, God, and then, at the end, when he had asked if there were any more skeletons, she had blithely told him no...!

'Arnold's a very good friend of my mother's,' she heard Hunter answer through the roaring in her ears. 'And he was also my father-in-law.'

Anne went cold, her whole being going into defensive shutdown against the pain.

Hunter had an intimate, long-standing connection with Arnold Markham. His reference to him had held friendly affection and deep respect. It was clear in which direction his loyalties would lie if it came to the crunch. Even as his lover, Anne would never have the hold on him that his beloved Deborah had.

Anne was going to have to make one, final sacrifice for her sister.

She was going to have to cram that last, leering skeleton back into the closet and firmly shut the door.

CHAPTER TEN

'YOU look a little frazzled, Anne; are you OK?' Rachel Blake asked as she opened the door of her sporty red convertible, parked conveniently close to the university library from which they had both just emerged.

Anne halted on the footpath, and sighed. 'Ever hear the phrase living on borrowed time?'

'Want a lift home?' said Rachel sympathetically.

'What, the whole five hundred metres?' Anne grinned, looking down the street towards the warehouse façade. She shook her head. 'Thanks anyway, Rach, but I'm fine—really. I'm just glad we break up for the holidays next week. I've got some serious lazing to do!'

Rachel took the hint cheerfully and Anne waved as the red car took off with its customary throaty roar. She was grateful for her friend's support but didn't see the point in another re-hash of the problem that she had blurted out one night after a few too many drinks at a wine bar while celebrating the end of a course assignment. Typically, Rachel, sophisticated to the core, had thought it a terrific lark, and strongly advised Anne to let sleeping dogs lie and make hay while the sun shone, along with numerous other applicable clichés.

'Why borrow trouble?' she had demanded. 'For all you know he might already have dumped you by the time he finds out, then you won't care what he thinks anyway.'

'Gee, thanks, Rachel, that makes me feel a lot better,' Anne had replied sarcastically. The fact that she and Professor Lewis were a hot item had quickly filtered around the campus in spite of their mutual discretion, but not even to Rachel had Anne admitted that she was in love, not lust.

'Or *you* might have dumped *him*,' Rachel had hastened to add consolingly. 'It's much more likely that you'll get bored with him than vice versa. After all, he's years older than you and you said he hardly ever takes you anywhere...'

Only to heaven and back. Who needed to party when they had a free ticket on a nightly ride to paradise?

But Rachel's flawed philosophy had held out an alluring appeal to someone whose conscience was already compromised, and as the weeks had slid by Anne had discovered the truth of Francis Bacon's axiom that it was impossible to love and be wise. She'd temporarily given up her idea of a part-time job and had cut down on her massages, purely on the off-chance of spending a few more precious hours a week with Hunter, and in consequence was dipping even more deeply into her precious savings.

It had certainly not been wisdom that had prompted her to phone her sister—not for news of Ivan, who had just cut his eighth tooth, or to find out that Dmitri, now somewhere on the high seas between Fiji and Hawaii, had been told that his residency application was being fast-tracked through the normally prolonged consideration process—but to beg for permission to draw Hunter into their confidence.

When she had confessed the reason, Katlin had been so depressingly brave that Anne had known as soon as she had hung up the phone that she couldn't do it.

'I guess you have to tell him, then, if it really means that much to you,' Katlin's voice had run hollowly down the line. 'I'll have to forfeit the publishing deal but, as long as they don't blacklist me, maybe I can hawk the book around to another editor... And maybe Dmitri'll be able to lend me some money to refund the grant if they threaten to sue... if he decides to stay, of course,'

she'd added cautiously. 'I don't want him to feel obli-
gated or anything. But—hey, maybe you're wrong and
it won't come to that!' Katlin pretending to be an optimist had not been very inspiring. 'Maybe you'll end
up finding out that Hunter's so much in love with you
that he's willing to be your accessory after the fact to
anything short of murder! Maybe if he thought he could
keep you by keeping his mouth shut...'

There were a few too many 'maybe's for Anne. The
only thing worse than Hunter *not* being in love with her
was the thought that his loving her would cause him pain.
How could she ask him to surrender his honour for her
sake? What had she done to earn such a sacrifice? It
would be a betrayal of her own love even to ask. Love
wasn't supposed to be a test. You didn't pass or fail.
Love was all about giving, not taking...

If giving was a measure of love then perhaps Hunter
wasn't as immune as he pretended to be, thought Anne
later as she let herself into his flat with the ingredients
for him to make another of his mouth-watering Italian
dishes, and found a huge wrapped package waiting for
her on the marble bench. Hunter was addicted to gift-
giving, which was a strange quirk in a man who had
insisted that she should not expect anything of him.

As well as the slim leather satchel that had replaced
her scruffy varsity book-bag, Hunter had surprised her
with clothes...pretty, extravagant things that she couldn't
possibly have afforded herself—the vibrant red dress she
was wearing now, a hot pink padded jacket that made
her easy to spot in a crowd, a Chinese robe that he had
acquired on his travels abroad, and which he liked her
to wear around the flat knowing she was naked underneath, some cobwebby underwear—and numerous frivolous trinkets including a not so frivolous Walkman radio
so that her love of loud rock music didn't clash with his
equal reverence for jazz and silence.

In turn she had given him the only thing of real value that she had to give—the secret gift of her love. If, as she suspected, Hunter was afraid to love again then *she* would be fearless. So she made herself vulnerable to him in a hundred small ways, respecting his periods of physical and mental withdrawal but making it quietly clear that she wasn't about to curb her natural warm exuberance in order to conform to his rigid concepts of mutual independence. She laughed at the shadow of rejection, challenged his cynicism with her enchantingly fresh view of the world, made him chuckle with her wit and impressed him with her fierce enthusiasm for the languages that she was learning by leaps and bounds, and her intense curiosity about the cultures they represented. She danced for him and taught him to appreciate the finer points of rap music, allowed him to inform her about art and politics and the subtleties of accepting defeat on the chessboard...

They now spent more evenings together than apart although they rarely slept together, separate beds seeming to be, to Hunter's incomprehensible way of thinking, an important factor in maintaining the necessary degree of emotional separation between lovers. Whenever he casually invited her to stay the entire night, Anne made herself accept just as casually, careful not to let him see her inward elation at the widening chink in his armour of assumed indifference.

The only real no-go area that Anne was solely responsible for, purely as a matter of self-defence, was her writing. If Hunter tried to discuss the book she bluntly changed the subject and, under his own rules, he was powerless to insist. Of course, not talking or thinking about it didn't make the constant dread of discovery go away and sometimes she caught him looking at her with a brooding speculation that made her heart shudder with apprehension.

The new gift was a silk floor-cushion in jewel-bright patchwork fabric—Hunter was well-acquainted with her preference for doing everything on the floor—and Anne immediately cast it on the carpet beside his favourite leather chair and looked for something to do on it while she waited for him to arrive home from his lecture. First, though, she had a shower and put on the peacock-blue Chinese robe, brushing her hair and leaving it rippling down her back, idly noticing the battered suitcase standing in the corner of his bedroom and wondering wistfully whether he might be emptying some space in his wardrobe for her. Carefully removing the long hairs from his brush, she put it back on the top of his chest of drawers and went out to raid his crammed bookcase, skipping her finger along the rows, stiffening as she suddenly came across a familiar name on a slender spine.

Deborah Markham Lewis.

She withdrew the slim volume and discovered that it was a book of poetry. She backed away, turning it over in her hands, slowly, as if it were primed to explode in her face. On the back cover was a large, full-length black and white photograph and underneath a few brief, biographical details.

'Poet...author...married to fellow author...published posthumously...'

Anne subsided on the cushion, staring at the photograph.

She had been right. Hunter's wife was beautiful, in the most classical sense of the word.

It was a fragile, ethereal, ultra-feminine beauty... the perfect, pale oval face, the floating Pre-Raphaelite hair, the cool intellect revealed by the light eyes, the delicate limbs under the flowing white dress...no wonder she haunted Hunter. She must have been his ideal intellectual as well as feminine mate!

She frowned as she turned the stiff pages, struggling with the incorporation of typographical elements into the unrhymed metre and the esoteric subject matter. Anne was no literary judge of poetry but she knew what she liked and Deborah Markham Lewis left her cold.

'What are you reading?'

She hadn't even heard him come in.

Hunter discarded his briefcase and came towards her, loosening his tie, his dark eyes smiling at the sight of her curled on the cushion, the Chinese silk cascading like a thin veil of water across her body. 'I see you like my present... it's called a harem pillow. As soon as I saw it in the shop window I imagined you waiting for me just as you are...'

She knew the exact moment when he recognised the book in her hand. His face seemed to draw in on itself, his lids half drawing down over shuttered eyes.

'I didn't know your wife was a poet,' said Anne, striving to act naturally. If he'd left the book on the shelf he must have expected her to notice it eventually. She tried to think of a diplomatic comment. 'They're very... profound. She must have been a very interesting woman.'

He gave her his thoughtful, heavy-lidded look and then shocked her by smiling faintly.

'That was ultra-polite of you, Anne, and most non-committal for a woman who holds definite opinions about almost everything. You don't like Deborah's poetry, do you?'

Caught out, Anne blushed and he shocked her afresh by adding kindly, 'Don't worry, I never liked her later stuff much either.'

'I—I'm sure she was very good...' she stammered faintly, her romantic illusions about his perfect marriage beginning to crumble around her startled ears.

'Oh, she was. Once. She had an enormous early promise that was never fulfilled... sound familiar?'

She ignored the wry tag, turning over the book and looking at the photograph with new eyes. 'She was very beautiful.'

'That was part of the problem,' he murmured cryptically, sliding his hand under her hair to stroke the sensitive nape of her neck.

Anne shivered, leaning her head back against his forearm so that she had an upside-down image of his face. 'What problem?' she asked, not expecting him to answer.

His hand stilled, then resumed its caress. 'She was used to being admired and flattered. She was an only child, an exquisitely elfin baby who grew into a stunning girl genius who grew into a beautiful, frightened woman. She had an image of perfection for herself that had to be maintained at all costs...'

A light went on inside Anne's head at the thought of that fey, wraith-like figure. She ducked her head and squirmed around to face him. 'Did Deborah have anorexia?'

His smile twisted as he crouched down beside her and took the book out of her hands, tossing it on to his chair. 'Clever Anne. Bulimia nervosa. But she was far too intelligent to let it control her. She apparently had it from her mid-teens but she hid it so well that I didn't know anything about it until it became useful to her to let me know.'

'Useful, how?'

He sat on the carpet, shrugging out of his jacket, the object of her rapt attention as he continued his casual revelations. She hardly dared breathe in case he suddenly realised whom he was talking to and clammed up again.

'To make me feel guilty, to stop me from pressuring her, I suppose.' He removed his cuff-links and rolled them absently around in his palm. 'Although at the time I thought I was just helping her. We had each had one book published when we met—I was lecturing at Victoria

University in Wellington—and it was a case of instant mutual fascination. But when we got married Deborah found that domesticity was vastly different from what she had imagined it should be for a "literary couple". She had a few short stories and a book of poems published in the first couple of years but she gradually started discarding most of what she wrote, endlessly rewriting the same piece only to decide it wasn't good enough.

'So she started to lie about how much work she was doing, first to other people, then to me and finally to herself, because failure didn't fit in with her image. Her output dropped pretty well in inverse proportion to mine, and inevitably she resented the fact that I was being published and she wasn't—quite rightly so, since she was the greater talent, according to the literary critics. Of course, she was a "serious" writer and I was an unashamed populist so there wasn't really any comparison, but she claimed my ego was afraid of the competition. Perhaps she was right and there was a subconscious rivalry I was never aware of. She said I was stifling her with my attention, that my criticism destroyed her self-confidence, that I frightened her with my temper and my sexual appetites.'

Anne was dazed. 'She said all *that*?' About *Hunter*? *Her* Hunter?

Hunter let the cuff-links roll to the floor and fingered the wide sash of her robe. 'Oh, much more than that; I'm just hitting the highlights,' he said drolly. 'But not all at once...it came out in dribs and drabs over the years as the bitterness built up. It got so that she couldn't bear to live with me, but she didn't dare live without me either, because I was her best excuse for failure. Her dreams had all gone sour and she had nothing to replace them with...only that incredible beauty. But she knew that was transient too...'

His face was remote but Anne knew him well enough by now to recognise that his rigid composure was indicative of internal turmoil. 'Was that when her bulimia got out of hand?'

'No.' Her question shook him out of his state of suspended animation, throwing a mental switch, and he suddenly tugged at the sash he was holding and Anne gasped, catching at the knot at her waist as she felt it begin to give.

'Shall we try the cushion out for size?' he said with soft lechery, as if they hadn't just been talking about a cataclysmic event in his life.

'I thought you were going to make dinner?' she murmured, to give herself time to think. Surely he couldn't expect her simply to ignore his intimate revelations? He must have told her for a purpose. But what was it?

'We can send out for pizza later.' He gave a sharper tug so that she almost slithered into his lap. 'You might show a little more enthusiasm. Or should I say a *lot* more...? That cushion was *extremely* expensive...'

That caught her on the raw, acutely conscious as she was of their financial disparity. Was he implying that her love was for sale? Did he know what an insult that was? 'I didn't realise you looked on it as an investment rather than a gift.' She lifted her chin and flashed her eyes at him warningly. 'Maybe if you show me the receipt I can work out how many kisses it's worth!'

'If you're talking fair exchange you might consider offering me that painting of mine that my mother gave you by mistake.' It had become a joke between them, his trying to bargain it away from her just as his mother had predicted, but this time Anne didn't respond and he shrugged.

'Well, it's definitely more than a few measly kisses,' he said smoothly. 'I'd say you owe me an orgasm at least...' His hand slipped inside the wrapped edge of the robe, and insolently between her legs.

She jerked to her knees, slapping his offensive hand away, glaring at him angrily, her breasts heaving against the twin embroidered dragons on their background of peacock silk as she sparked to his outrageous challenge. How could such an intelligent man be so utterly *insensitive*? she wondered.

His eyes lit with a sultry triumph at her reaction and it suddenly hit her what he was doing, what he always did as a prelude to their lovemaking...

'Oh, no, you're not going to get away with it this time!' she said, forcing herself to relax back on her heels and drop her defensive posture.

'Get away with what?' he said, still with that same, darkly mocking expression.

'Tormenting me. Starting an argument. That's what you do, isn't it, as part of your seduction routine? You never just take me in your arms to make love. You try to tip me off balance first. You say something deliberately to annoy me, or you tease me until I lash back. Why?'

He shrugged and stated with ungracious bluntness, 'Adrenalin is a great aphrodisiac.'

'I don't need any aphrodisiacs around you,' she countered steadily. 'You must know by now you can turn me on with a look. And you certainly don't seem to have any trouble getting aroused.' She directed a pointed look at his lap. 'So why does sex always have to start out as a battle, Hunter? What are you afraid of? It's something to do with Deborah, isn't it? About the way she died...'

His eyes narrowed at her insistence. 'I don't want to talk about it any more.'

But he did. It was burning inside him. She could see that clearly now for the first time. Good God, while she had been busy tiptoeing around the edges of his forbidden zones, had he been *wanting* her to force him to this point?

'Well, that's just too bad,' she told him hotly, taking the gamble of her life. 'You're going to! For once *I'm* making the rules around here and rule number one is that if you start something you damned well finish it. How did she die, Hunter?'

'What's the matter, Anne? Do you think I killed her?' he murmured with an embittered sarcasm.

'No! But I think *you* think you did.'

Her quiet words brought a violent release.

'Oh, no, she definitely killed herself...while I was away overseas on a research trip. ODed on antidepressants—because there's no danger of damaging your looks that way,' he added with a bitterness that fended off her shocked compassion. 'No, intellectually I know I didn't kill her. However, I also know that our marriage was a disaster for her. But for my falling in love with her and convincing her to marry me, Deborah would be alive today, perhaps fulfilling that glorious potential of hers in the way that she was meant to...'

'You can't know that—if she had bulimia she already had latent problems——'

'Yes, but I can't deny the excellent probability that our marriage triggered them into full-blown depression. She left a note, you see, explaining why life wasn't worth living any more. It was because she had realised that she didn't have any life... there was only mine, slowly eating her up, growing fat and bloated off her weakness and dependence—a loathsomely vivid image for a bulimic. It was quite a brilliant little note, concise, fluid, emotionally wrenching. It's ironic that some of her most powerful writing in years was in her suicide note...'

He took a harsh breath. 'She said that I had paralysed her talent with constant emotional and physical demands, because I was jealous of her talent and obsessed with dominating every sphere of her existence. The only way she felt she could reclaim total control over her destiny was by dying. Divorce obviously didn't occur to her as a possible alternative,' he said aridly.

'She was ill, I'm not,' said Anne, softly drawing his attention away from the painful memories. 'You don't have to keep warning me about your dominating temperament. I got that message right from day one and it doesn't frighten me. I'm not a reincarnation of Deborah. I'm *nothing* like her.'

'I know.' He picked up a lock of her hair and let it trail down over her breast, with a faint, whimsical smile. 'Oh, *God*, I know . . . you're more sensual than cerebral. You make a celebration out of life . . .'

'Nothing like her at all,' she repeated resolutely. 'I'm physically strong, for one thing. And I come from a big family, so I'm used to rough-and-tumble emotions and to asserting myself against bullying. Just because I love you it doesn't mean I've undergone a personality transplant——'

'Anne——'

'I'm still me. I'm not going to fall apart if you love me back . . . or if you leave me.' She looked him dead in the eye. 'I certainly don't have Deborah's hang-ups about my artistic talent being smothered by yours——'

'Anne——'

'Because there's nothing to smother. I don't have any great literary aspirations——'

His hand suddenly clamped over her mouth. 'Enough,' he warned.

'No, not enough,' she said in a voice muffled by the press of his warm palm. 'I don't *want* to be a writer, Hunter. I never did——'

'I said *enough*!' He was laughing. He took his hand away, and she was suddenly speechless at the tenderness of his expression as he clasped her wrist and drew it over his lips in a feather-light caress.

'I don't want to argue with you,' he went on with a husky intonation that made her body react with delicious recognition. 'I want to take you in my arms and make long, slow, rapturous love with you . . .'

He picked up and kissed her other wrist. 'Would you like to do that with me, Anne?' He gently touched her brow, her lips, her heart . . . his fingers curving delicately under her breast. She was stunned by the open adoration in his sensuous invitation. 'I can be tender with you, darling; I can be anything you want . . .' He leaned forward and kissed her parted mouth, his own warm and mellow, his tongue curling pliantly around hers, mating languidly with it until she began to tremble. 'Give me this chance to show you how sweetly we can entwine together . . .' he whispered thickly, his mouth moving on to cherish her throat, his hands flowing over her like warm honey, enticing them both with soft forays under the edges of the blue silk. 'I can make this even more exciting for you than the other way . . .' he promised bewitchingly. 'Not as instantly electrifying perhaps, but more powerfully erotic and just as intoxicating in the end . . .'

Sixteen hours after the most earth-shattering proof of that promise Anne was deep in the throes of an entirely different kind of intoxication, shaking with a delirium of outraged fury as she read the letter that she had found on her doormat when she'd arrived back from her morning lecture.

The coward had run away!

On paper Hunter spouted a lot of phrases about their both 'needing this time apart to reassess their priorities' and his not wanting to take advantage of her 'soft heart' and her 'dangerous habit of self-sacrifice'. He thought that at this time in her life she should be concentrating on pursuing her own dreams instead of continually setting them aside for the sake of others, him included.

But what it all boiled down to was that Hunter hadn't had the guts to say goodbye to her face. He must have planned this extended research trip for weeks, probably *months*, and yet even on the brink of departure he had said nothing about going away. It had been his secret escape-hatch and her passionate declaration of love last night had sent him bolting smartly through it. Perhaps his reticence had been a superstitious hangover from the tragic way his marriage had ended during a similar overseas trip, but Anne was in no mood to give him the benefit of the doubt. Probably he had just wanted to avoid a scene!

'I am *not* Deborah!' she screamed futilely to the empty air, ripping his Dear Anne missive to shreds and then shakily trying to piece it back together a few minutes later in order to try and read between the lines. He hadn't even bothered to write it by hand. His kiss-off letter was typewritten, like a page from one of his novels, and signed simply 'Hunter'. Not 'Best wishes' or 'Regards' or 'Till we meet again'. And, glaringly obvious, not 'Love'...

The most unforgivable thing of all was his destination. While Anne spent three weeks rattling around her flat in wintry August with no classes and no job because she had assumed that she and Hunter would be spending the time together, *he* was going to be swanning around Russia. *Russia*! The one country in the world that she would most love to visit! He couldn't have calculated a greater insult to her humiliating injury.

When she found out from one of his fellow lecturers that Hunter had two months' leave it was the last straw, and Anne did what any heartbroken, well brought up girl did in a crisis.

She went home to Mum.

Fortunately she managed to hitch a ride as far as Wellington with a student relative of Rachel's who was returning home for the holidays, a nice, gangly boy whose idea of conversation, to her relief, was singing along to heavy metal tapes played at full volume in the stereo on wheels that passed for his car.

At Wellington Anne caught the Cook Strait Ferry and stood on the deck in the biting wind hunched into the jacket Hunter had given her, staring out at the white-capped grey waters between the two islands of New Zealand and wondering what wonderful experiences he was having without her. And what if they weren't so wonderful? What if he got somehow caught up in the internal politics of the former Soviet states? What if he got hurt or went missing? What if he was waylaid by a ravishingly beautiful, karate-kicking former KGB agent with big breasts and emotions of pure steel—all his unreasonable macho fantasies come true. He would probably have her tied to his bed in no time!

At Picton her brother Don met her in the family station wagon and there was another two hours of driving before they reached the farm, where Anne was finally free to sob out her misery on her mother's ample breast and accept a warm soothing of maternal outrage spiced with womanly understanding.

After a week being fussed over and cossetted like an invalid, Anne was shooed off to the coast to visit Katlin and Ivan, and she found Dmitri there, finally out of his officer's whites and temporarily employed by a local yacht charter company. After she had marvelled dutifully at Ivan's miraculous new ability to walk, she had a quiet session with Katlin and was relieved to be told that she was on to the last chapter of her book. Then she took Ivan down to the beach to dig in the sand and catch up on her news, specifically about that lovely man next door who had turned out to be a snake in the grass. Ivan nodded sagely at this, as if he had suspected it all along, and consolingly pushed a fistful of sand into her down-turned mouth.

Over lunch Dmitri dropped his bombshell, gravely thanking her for her vital assistance with his residency application, which seemed certain now to be approved.

When she protested she hadn't done anything he corrected her.

'Yes, you have, for without your Professor Lewis things would be going much more slowly. He has cut through much officialdom in Russian Foreign Service by using his contacts here, and in Russia.'

'*Hunter* did? But how? Why?'

'He does it for you, perhaps? Because he knows your family means much to you. He left a message with my shipping company that he wants to help and they passed it on to me...'

Two weeks later, back in Auckland preparing for a new term, Anne was still fuming about what she had found out. If Hunter had involved himself in Dmitri's application, then he must have seen the form which identified the mother of Dmitri's son as one Katlin Clare Tremaine of Golden Bay, and the biographical information that mentioned a sister named, Anne, a student, in Auckland.

No *wonder* he had finally stopped nagging her about her so-called book. No wonder he had seduced her into shutting up that last night! He didn't *need* her confession, he knew already. She had been dragging around that great burden of guilt for goodness' knows how long for *nothing*! And all that 'you have to pursue dreams' stuff in the letter had obviously been his subtle and miserably apt revenge.

But if he knew, then at least he hadn't informed on her and Kat...yet. There had been not a peep from the grants people. Perhaps he hadn't had time before he left. Perhaps he intended to hold the threat over her head when he returned, she thought with a frisson of excitement...to blackmail her into his bed. Or more likely, she decided glumly, to keep her out of it!

She was thinking just such dark thoughts on the last Saturday before term, walking up an inner-city side-street from the department store where she had just landed herself a weekend job. Gusts of wind were blowing the rain across the footpath, wetting her woollen leggings, and she glanced through the glass frontage of a hotel café, envying the people tucked snugly inside, and came to a dead halt. She leaned over and pressed her face against the window-pane, ignoring the glare of the waitress inside.

Hunter!

The man who was supposed to be steeping himself in the mysteries of Russian politics was sitting calmly in an Auckland café laughing and sipping drinks with an elegant male companion who looked as if he had just stepped from the pages of *Gentleman's Quarterly*. He was back in Auckland and hadn't bothered to let her know!

Anne didn't stop to think. She slammed open the door and marched over to their table. Hunter and his guest looked up in surprise as she opened her mouth and let fly.

During her few days at Golden Bay, Dmitri had given Anne some personal coaching in Russian conversation, recording some tapes which she had brought back with her and humorously complying with her request to teach her some pithy nautical phrases and insulting slang, some of which he had refused to give her literal translations for, claiming it was too obscene. She used them all now, with great relish, telling Hunter exactly what she thought of his worthless character and criminal antecedents and finally, wildly, accusing him of planning the whole trip to Russia for the sole purpose of punishing her for daring to get too close.

When she paused for her first breath Hunter, who had folded his arms and bowed his arrogant head with every indication of penitent shame, raised mocking eyes and said blandly, in crisp English, 'It's wonderful to see you too, Anne. I'd like you to meet my very good friend of many years, Alexei Danilov. Alexei is a professor of

English at Moscow University. We arrived on the same flight together this morning and I offered to help settle him into his hotel before we parted ways. It's his first time in New Zealand and first impressions are so important, don't you think? Alexei, this is the lady I've been boring you about.'

'Oh, no!' Anne sank down into the empty chair that Hunter coolly thrust out with his ox-blood shoe and covered her mortified face with her hands. And she had thought she was being so clever, spitting out her temper at Hunter in a language she thought only the two of them would understand!'

'Delighted to meet you, Anne,' said the suave stranger in a voice that held a low quiver. 'And may I say that you're a great deal more accomplished in my language than my friend here has led me to believe.'

'Unless I miss my guess, she's been consorting with sailors... or at least, one sailor in particular,' Hunter said slyly. 'Dmitri is such a wonderful *fund* of information, isn't he, Anne?'

She refused to lift her face from its grateful hiding place. 'You're not supposed to be here—what are you doing here?' she said into her cupped hands. 'You're away for another six weeks.'

'I reassessed my priorities more quickly than I expected.' His wry reply gained him the reaction he sought. She peeped hopefully at him through her fingers and he pounced. 'Invented any good fiction lately? Anne considers herself something of a budding author, Alexei...'

His sarcasm made her burn and Anne's hands crashed to the table, making cutlery and crockery jump. 'No, I don't! You know damned well it was Katlin, not me, who won that grant. I can't write for peanuts!'

'Mmm, your skills are definitely more in the verbal line,' agreed Hunter silkily. 'You're a fierce little liar when your protective instincts have been aroused.'

She should have been furious with him but, looking into those deep black eyes, she was suddenly overwhelmed with love. His hair was a little longer and his skin a shade darker than when she had last seen him, but otherwise he was very much the lover of her fevered dreams.

'How long have you known?'

'About your pretending to be Katlin? For certain, only a few days before I left, when I saw Dmitri's humanitarian grounds documentation—I used it in Moscow to circumvent the system and get certified copies of his educational and medical records from sympathetic records clerks. But I'd already had a hunch there was something strange about you and that book. You seemed far too blasé about your first novel. You just didn't seem to have a real writer's *temperament*...'

'You mean selfish and cynical and sullen and suspicious and always believing the worst of people?'

'You certainly thought the worst of *me*. Did you think I made a habit of seducing innocent virgins and then throwing them to the wolves? Damn it, Anne—you gave all your loyalty to your family, even to Dmitri who was a complete stranger—and none of it to me! You can't blame me for storming off in a snit.'

Anne tried not to notice Alexei's amused interest. 'Yes, well . . . you acted pretty callously sometimes. You were always pushing me away. And how could you not tell me you were going away for two months!'

'I was too busy whistling in the dark. I was afraid that my judgement was becoming impaired by the intensity of my feelings—as it had been when I met Deborah—so I proved that it wasn't by functioning in that part of my life in which you weren't already involved as if you didn't exist.

'But you do exist, and all I proved was my folly in believing that I could control passion and love in the same way that I controlled fear and bad memories—by ignoring them.'

'But in that letter——'

'Oh, I believed everything that I wrote...at the time,' he added the self-derisive qualifier. 'Especially the bit about self-sacrifice. All those years you cared for your mother and family you dreamed those secret dreams of travel and adventure and a challenging international career. You'd *earned* the right to those dreams, Anne, the hard way. I had no right even to think of asking you to put them aside again, perhaps forever, in favour of *my* idea of paradise—a home and children, and equal partnership—the kind of ties that bind forever. I had one relationship which was destroyed by conflicting careers and broken dreams, I didn't think I could face another...'

'Oh, and *I* thought the letter was being sarcastic about my dreams of being an author,' Anne blurted out in relief, a star-burst of happiness forming in her breast. She shrugged happily. 'That roving translator thing...it's not set in concrete, you know. It's only one of so many wonderful *possibilities*. Who knows what I might turn out to be best at by the time I graduate? Whether I might rather teach, or start my own language school... And people do travel with children, you know. Nowhere does it say that babies have to be chained forever to their birthplace—travel is very broadening for the young mind...'

He rolled his eyes. 'You're doing it already. Don't be so bloody *accommodating*——'

'I can if I want to, that's what freedom of choice is all about,' she said tartly. He loved her, and she was going to make him admit it if she had to arm-wrestle him to the floor. 'I can be as accommodating as I like and no one can stop me!'

'Least of all me. Yes, I finally managed to work that out. But I was so caught up with my noble act of self-sacrifice that it took me a few miserable weeks to realise that I was doing exactly what I had walked away to *stop* myself from doing—denying you your right to choose freely your own destiny. For better or worse. So, Anne…'

He paused and looked around the crowded, noisy café with a pained expression before he turned back, visibly composing himself.

'Yes, Hunter?' Anne asked innocently.

From the corner of her eye she saw Alexei, chin on hand, watching in amusement as his big, bullish, fearsomely confident friend toyed with a spoon, shifted the vase in the middle of the table left and then right again, and cleared his throat.

'Alexei says that St Petersburg in springtime is a lovely place for a honeymoon.'

Anne's eyes suddenly stung as she looked at him, the square chin and the mouth that had cut at her a hundred times, and kissed her even more. She struggled for her ragged breath. She would begin as she meant to carry on…

'If you're asking me to marry you, Hunter Lewis, you'd better do it right, so there's no misunderstanding about it later! I would hate you to accuse me of *assuming* that you had proposed when you were just making an idle comment on the tourism industry…'

His answer was to pluck a ring from his pocket and the red rose from the vase on the table and present them to her with a smoulderingly aggressive look.

'You want me to be more explicit. All right. I love you and I know damned well you love me, so will you please drive me crazy for the rest of my life by marrying me, Anne Tremaine? and giving me children and helping me raise them, and dragging me around the world at your heels whenever you get the restless urge to stray?'

'I do believe the only correct response to such a question in the circumstances is—*Da*,' translated their fascinated witness with a deep chuckle.

Anne looked at Hunter, so brightly expectant, so intense, and yet mellowed with the merest hint of male complacency. Hunter's belief in the strength and the quality of her love was so complete that he had always known what her answer would be.

And it would be no sacrifice to give it, wholeheartedly and without reservation.

The temptation was utterly irresistible.

She lowered her lashes demurely.

'I'll think about it,' she said sweetly.

She was on her feet and out of the door, laughing, before the vibration of Hunter's outraged roar became sound in her ears.

He caught her ten metres up the footpath, leaving Alexei to foot the bill. And it took him all of ten seconds to get the answer he wanted.

BRIDE'S BAY RESORT

UNLOCK THE DOOR TO GREAT ROMANCE AT BRIDE'S BAY RESORT

Join Harlequin's new across-the-lines series, set in an exclusive hotel on an island off the coast of South Carolina.

Seven of your favorite authors will bring you exciting stories about fascinating heroes and heroines discovering love at Bride's Bay Resort.

Look for these fabulous stories coming to a store near you beginning in January 1996.

Harlequin American Romance #613 in January
Matchmaking Baby by Cathy Gillen Thacker

Harlequin Presents #1794 in February
Indiscretions by Robyn Donald

Harlequin Intrigue #362 in March
Love and Lies by Dawn Stewardson

Harlequin Romance #3404 in April
Make Believe Engagement by Day Leclaire

Harlequin Temptation #588 in May
Stranger in the Night by Roseanne Williams

Harlequin Superromance #695 in June
Married to a Stranger by Connie Bennett

Harlequin Historicals #324 in July
Dulcie's Gift by Ruth Langan

Visit Bride's Bay Resort each month wherever Harlequin books are sold.

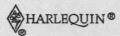

HARLEQUIN®

BBAYG

HARLEQUIN  PRESENTS®

Don't be late for the wedding!

Be sure to make a date in your diary for the happy event—
The eighth in our tantalizing new selection of stories...

Wedlocked!

Bonded in matrimony, torn by desire...

Coming next month:

THE VALENTINE CHILD by Jacqueline Baird
Harlequin Presents #1795

Bestselling author of *Nothing Changes Love*

Valentine was the son Justin Gifford didn't know he had.
Zoe, Justin's wife, was determined to keep Justin out of her
baby's life.... Then Valentine needed help and Zoe knew
she'd do anything for him...anything at all....even if it meant
she'd have to *seduce* her *own husband!*

Available in February wherever Harlequin books are sold.